A MI▯
BARBARA CARTLAND

Barbaracartland.com Ltd

.com

POD Preparation by M-Y Books
m-ybooks.co.uk

THE BARBARA CARTLAND PINK COLLECTION

Barbara Cartland was the most prolific bestselling author in the history of the world. She was frequently in the Guinness Book of Records for writing more books in a year than any other living author. In fact her most amazing literary feat was when her publishers asked for more Barbara Cartland romances, she doubled her output from 10 books a year to over 20 books a year, when she was 77.

She went on writing continuously at this rate for 20 years and wrote her last book at the age of 97, thus completing 400 books between the ages of 77 and 97.

Her publishers finally could not keep up with this phenomenal output, so at her death she left 160 unpublished manuscripts, something again that no other author has ever achieved.

Now the exciting news is that these 160 original unpublished Barbara Cartland books are ready for publication and they will be published by Barbaracartland.com exclusively on the internet, as the web is the best possible way to reach so many Barbara Cartland readers around the world.

The 160 books will be published monthly and will be numbered in sequence.

The series is called the Pink Collection as a tribute to Barbara Cartland whose favourite colour was pink and it became very much her trademark over the years.

The Barbara Cartland Pink Collection is published only on the internet. Log on to www.barbaracartland.com to find out how you can purchase the books monthly as they are published, and take out a subscription that will ensure that all subsequent editions are delivered to you by mail order to your home.

TITLES IN THIS SERIES

THE LATE DAME BARBARA CARTLAND

Barbara Cartland, who sadly died in May 2000 at the grand age of ninety eight, remains one of the world's most famous romantic novelists. With worldwide sales of over one billion, her outstanding 723 books have been translated into thirty six different languages, to be enjoyed by readers of romance globally.

Writing her first book "Jigsaw" at the age of 21, Barbara became an immediate bestseller. Building upon this initial success, she wrote continuously throughout her life, producing bestsellers for an astonishing 76 years. In addition to Barbara Cartland's legion of fans in the UK and across Europe, her books have always been immensely popular in the USA. In 1976 she achieved the unprecedented feat of having books at numbers 1 & 2 in the prestigious B. Dalton Bookseller bestsellers list.

Although she is often referred to as the "Queen of Romance", Barbara Cartland also wrote several historical biographies, six autobiographies and numerous theatrical plays as well as books on life, love, health and cookery. Becoming one of Britain's most popular media personalities and dressed in her trademark pink, Barbara spoke on radio and television about social and political issues, as well as making many public appearances.

In 1991 she became a Dame of the Order of the British Empire for her contribution to literature and her work for humanitarian and charitable causes.

Known for her glamour, style, and vitality Barbara Cartland became a legend in her own lifetime. Best remembered for her wonderful romantic novels and loved by millions of readers worldwide, her books remain treasured for their heroic heroes, plucky heroines and traditional values. But above all, it was Barbara Cartland's overriding belief in the positive power of love to help, heal and improve the quality of life for everyone that made her truly unique.

*"When I fell in love with the love of my life, I fervently
believed that I had been blessed by God and that our
love would go on for ever – not just for this life but for
many other lives yet to come into Eternity.
And you know what – I was right!"*

Barbara Cartland

CHAPTER ONE
1845

Prince Nicolo of Vienz rode his horse up to the front door of the Palace and dismounted.

There was a moment's pause before a groom came running from the direction of the stables.

"Your Royal Highness be back here early," he said breathlessly.

"Yes, I know," the Prince replied, "but I think this horse is going lame on its left leg. Tell Petre to see to it."

"Very good, Your Royal Highness."

The groom took the horse slowly away and the Prince walked into the Palace.

"Your Royal Highness is back early," one of the equerries piped up, having hurried into the hall when he saw him appear.

"As I have already been told," the Prince answered rather sharply. "Where is Her Royal Highness?"

"She is in the garden, Sire. I think Comte Ruta is showing Her Royal Highness the lake."

The Prince nodded.

He walked towards the side of the Palace which led into the garden, thinking as he did so that he should last night have suggested to the Princess that she might like to ride with him in the morning.

He had been so bored over dinner that he had not actually considered what would happen the next day.

Princess Marziale of Bassanz had arrived yesterday with an entourage of Ladies-in-Waiting and a Countess to chaperone her.

The Prince had felt hostile from the very moment they stepped into the Palace.

He had fought against his Government, his relatives and even his own people in his determination not to marry.

Eventually because of the number of revolutions that had taken place in Principalities around him, he had yielded to the urgent request, as such a marriage would unite Bassanz – quite a large independent country – with his own and make them both stronger.

Vienz had managed to remain independent while revolutions or annexations had taken place in many States in that part of Northern Italy since the defeat of Napoleon.

The Prince had often thought it was Napoleon who had upset everything and so it was difficult for the smaller States and Principalities to continue on their own.

The larger countries bordering Vienz were greedy and Austria particularly had been a menace for a long time.

The Prince felt that his Prime Minister was being over-anxious and yet he was well aware that a tie between Vienz and Bassanz would surely make them both stronger.

At the same time he had no wish to marry anyone.

At twenty-seven he was enjoying life enormously.

On his father's death he had reigned for the last five years in Vienz and he had his own ideas and they were forceful ones of all he could do for his country.

He was very conscious that the people he ruled over admired him and were willing to follow him, but he had been obliged to listen to endless bleatings that he should marry and produce an heir and many younger sons.

"It is no use leaving it too long, my dearest," his grandmother had said with tears in her eyes. "Supposing something happens to you – although I pray to God it will not – you know as well as I do, there is no one competent to take your place."

"I am well aware of that," Prince Nicolo replied. "Equally I can hardly imagine any heir, if I had one, taking over the country and being able to rule it for at least the next twenty years."

He was speaking sarcastically but his grandmother added quite seriously,

"Of course the Prime Minister and the Cabinet will do that. But it would make sure of the continuity of our family. As you well know we have now reigned in Vienz for over three centuries."

"Hanging on at times by the skin of our teeth," the Prince countered jokingly.

However his grandmother still looked worried.

"I grant you there have been anxious moments, but the family has survived and that is what you must ensure for the future."

If it was not his grandmother, then it was the Prime Minister. He was very able but a nervous man who always anticipated the worst.

"I don't like what I hear is happening in Austria," he had said not just once but a hundred times to the Prince. "We are as strongly armed as it is possible to be, but one never knows what might happen."

"Of course we don't know," the Prince said rather irritably, "but our Army is enormous in comparison with other small independent countries and the Austrians are well aware of it."

"What we really need is that Your Royal Highness should take a wife. And on looking around I am certain that Princess Marziale has the most to offer you."

"I have never seen or met the Princess and I have no intention of marrying a 'pig in a poke'," the Prince replied caustically.

"She is reputed to be good-looking and charming, and she is also, I am reliably informed, very popular with her own people."

The Prince did not feel that was exactly what he desired in a wife and it would be a great mistake to raise the hopes of the ruling family of Bassanz and then cry off at the last moment.

But it was impossible for him to go on fighting.

Finally he had agreed to invite the Princess to stay at the Palace so they could at least get to know each other.

He had meant it to be a purely social visit, but then needless to say, the Prime Minister, all his relatives and everyone else of consequence in Vienz thought differently.

They looked on it as a direct suggestion from him to the Princess that they should be married although he protested that it was only to be a friendly meeting of two neighbours.

But the Statesmen on both sides assumed that the purpose of their meeting was to decide the date for their wedding.

The Prince felt he had been caught in a trap from which it was impossible to escape and his situation made him not only apprehensive but extremely bad-tempered.

He had enjoyed a number of *affaires-de-coeur* with charming women and they had known from the start that it was quite impossible for him to marry them.

And they had therefore enjoyed being with him, not because he was a Royal Prince, but because he was a very handsome man.

He for his part found that however attractive these women were sooner or later he grew bored with the liaison.

This was because he was exceptionally well-read and he therefore found it tiresome to be with a woman who never read anything but social gossip in the newspapers or a few rather sickly love stories.

He had gone from one casual love affair to another and by the time his family found out that there was a new face in the Palace, the lady in question had usually left the country.

'When I take a wife,' the Prince had often thought, 'I want someone I can talk to about the affairs of State and discuss the problems of keeping my own people happy and content.'

He rather doubted from what he had seen of the ruling families in other States that this was possible.

Of course he had been invited to stay with the other Rulers of neighbouring States, large and small, and he had found that most of them were extremely dull. Also he felt that they were not doing enough for their own people or for the development of their countries.

In the back of his mind was always the fear that Austria would gobble them up, as had happened to many smaller States in the past.

What was worse, the daughters of the Rulers who were paraded in front of him as soon as he arrived were in most cases dull, plain and badly educated young women.

It was of course a universal practice that the men must have the best education possible, while the daughters, both of Royalty or aristocracy, should be content with a governess, who knew little more than themselves.

The result was, the Prince found, that while the young Princesses looked at him with admiring eyes, they had nothing to contribute to the conversation nor had they any knowledge of what was happening in the world outside their own countries.

'How can it be possible,' the Prince used to ask himself as he went home, 'that I could listen day after day and year after year to such idiotic conversations as I have endured in the last few days?'

But when he returned to Vienz he had to listen again to the pleading that he should put a wedding ring on some plain but Royal young woman's finger.

Immediately, according to them, she would produce a brilliant heir. An heir who would follow him when he was no longer capable of ruling his country himself.

"The whole idea is rubbish from start to finish," the Prince raged, but no one would listen to him except his valet, who was paid to do so.

All his protests fell on deaf ears until finally he was forced to invite Princess Marziale to pay him a visit.

He tried to make it very clear it was only a matter of a friendly meeting and that there was no suggestion of anything more.

Yet everybody in the Palace then behaved as if the marriage was settled and it was only a matter of walking up the aisle at the Cathedral where the Archbishop would be waiting for them.

In fact as the Prince had to admit to himself the whole thing was now out of hand.

It was his fault for giving in in the first place and inviting the Princess against his will.

It had been a trap from the very beginning and now that he had stepped into it, it was going to be very hard to shake himself free.

He had waited apprehensively yesterday afternoon when the party from Bassanz was due to arrive.

He had to admit they did it in style. There were four closed carriages each drawn by a team of magnificent well-matched horses.

Princess Marziale, when she stepped out of the first carriage to draw up in front of the Palace, was, the Prince had to admit, quite pretty. She had dark hair and dark eyes and a perfect complexion.

She was of course dressed in a way that told him that whoever produced this show was certainly experienced at his job.

The Princess entered the Palace wearing a gown of rose pink and the feathers in her hat of the same shade.

She sank in a most elaborate curtsy in front of the Prince and he had to admit that she was playing her part exceedingly well.

"Welcome to Vienz," the Prince greeted her, "and I so hope Your Royal Highness will enjoy your stay here."

"I am sure I will," the Princess said in a soft voice. "I had no idea until I looked out of the windows of the carriage that your country is so beautiful."

"The same might be said of you," the Prince replied gallantly.

He noticed as he spoke that it was with the greatest difficulty that the Prime Minister and those beside him did not applaud.

They drank champagne to relieve the rigours of the journey and then the Princess walked up to the State rooms to change for dinner and the Prince to his own apartments.

Princess Marziale had said very little while they were drinking in the huge Reception room overlooking the garden, but the Prince had been suddenly aware of the Comte Ruta.

The Comte had gone on his orders to Bassanz to escort the Princess and her entourage over the border into Vienz and he had obviously primed her well as to what she should say and what she should do.

The Comte, as chief of his many *aides-de-camp*, was older than the others and very experienced in social behaviour. He had suggested a number of alterations in the Palace that the Prince thought were in very good taste.

He therefore deliberately chose the Comte to go to Bassanz as he was undoubtedly the right person to make it absolutely clear to the Princess that this was only a social visit and nothing more meaningful than that.

The Prince had insisted on the Comte going rather than leave it to the Prime Minister to choose an envoy, as if he did the Prince was quite certain that he would inform the Princess that she would receive a proposal of marriage before the visit ended.

The Prince thought with amusement that the Comte had doubtless rehearsed Princess Marziale on what she should say to him.

At dinner time he was even more certain of it.

She asked him about his horses.

And what he was doing for the young people in the Cities and if they had developed anything new in the way of industry.

The Prince knew when he replied to her questions that she was not really interested in the answers. They meant nothing to her.

At the same time he told himself it was a good effort on the Comte's part and he would congratulate him later on for being, if nothing else, a good tutor.

Again at the Comte's suggestion they danced after dinner. This was a change from sitting talking which the Prince usually preferred.

The band had obviously been instructed to provide new tunes for the dances and the Princess was a very good dancer and the Prince then 'opened the ball', as it might mockingly have been called, with her.

As everyone else took to the floor, they danced to a tune that had captivated Paris the previous year.

It made the Prince remember he had, at the time, been pursuing one of the most attractive *courtesans* in the Capital and she had not only been attractive in her own way but was also witty and amusing.

He had found himself laughing with her more than he had ever laughed in any other *affaire de coeur*.

But Princess Marziale was silent until the dance ended and then she said almost as if repeating her lesson,

"Your Royal Highness is a very good dancer."

"So are you, Princess."

"We don't have too many balls back at home, but I have been practising this last month."

He did not have to ask why. Doubtless someone had informed her that there would be dancing after dinner.

It seemed to him, when he went upstairs to bed, that the chains were being fastened around him and it would be quite impossible for him to find any fault with her as they undoubtedly anticipated he would.

When he said goodnight to her, the Princess had made what he felt certain was a well rehearsed speech.

She told him how much she was enjoying visiting Vienz and how thrilled she was with the Palace.

"Tomorrow," she insisted, "you really must show me your horses. I am told they are outstanding."

"I would like to think so," replied the Prince, "but of course when you arrived I saw that your horses were most splendidly matched."

Then the Comte had interposed, saying,

"Her Royal Highness's father only recently bought the horses that carried her here today. He acquired them because, as Your Royal Highness observed, they were so perfectly matched. It's not easy to find teams that size."

The Prince was acutely aware that the horses had been purchased just for this particular occasion.

After climbing into his bed he had laid awake for some time thinking about Princess Marziale.

It was difficult to find fault with her performance, but his intuition told him that it was just for his benefit and his benefit alone.

11

That they had taken such trouble in Bassanz made him suspicious and it increased his feeling of being caught in a trap.

When he had finally yielded to the urging of his Prime Minister and of his family and had invited Princess Marziale to the Palace, he had tried to make it absolutely clear that it did not commit him in any way.

But now he was feeling that he had been a fool to have given in to them.

What he should have done was to go to Bassanz himself, call on the Princess's father and quite casually meet the Princess while he did so – instead he had allowed the arrangements to be orchestrated by the Prime Minister.

He was now sure that in Bassanz they were waiting with bated breath to hear that the marriage was arranged.

'Why the hell did I get myself into this mess?' the Prince asked himself when he found it difficult to sleep.

*

In fact he rose early and rode off alone the moment he had eaten his breakfast.

He of course had to have a bodyguard of soldiers in attendance, but on his instructions they invariably kept a long way behind him so he did not have to talk to them.

If there was one thing that he really disliked it was people chattering away in the morning before he had time to think what he had to do during the day.

Because he had not slept well, he rode faster than usual and his bodyguard had difficulty keeping him in sight.

When he finally turned back, it was because he had a feeling that, if he stayed away from the Palace for too long, the Princess would be waiting to astound him with another performance the moment he returned.

It was still quite early and he had no appointments arranged for at least another hour.

The Prince rode up to the front door, dismounted and walked indoors.

He was told the Princess was in the garden and he thought that this was an excellent opportunity for him to talk to her sensibly.

He had already thought out what he would say and told himself that any woman would understand his feelings if he was tactful about it.

He would tell her that he had no wish to commit himself until such time as they both found they could get on well together.

'I will let her know what I expect of my wife,' he decided. 'If she does not like it, then we can acknowledge that the whole idea, which came not from us but from those who surround us, can be put aside outright.'

Even as he figured this out, he was certain that the Princess would be too scared of her parents not to accept his proposal if in fact he made it.

'What I have to do is to convince her that she must have a mind of her own and thus if she does not love me, it would be fatal for us to be married and have children.'

This idea had always been in his mind since he grew up.

He had known even when he enjoyed his *affaires-de-coeur* with *courtesans* and married women that this was not really what he wanted or should have.

He recognised only too well that for Princes in his position marriage was normally not a question of love – what really mattered was the benefit it would bring to the countries they ruled.

Equally he would have been very stupid, which he was not, if he had not realised that women found him extremely attractive.

When his *affaires-de-coeur* with them ended, there were usually tears and it was never a question of whether the woman would love him, but if he could love her.

'I want to love my wife,' he had thought during the night. 'I wish to love, adore and worship the mother of my children and in consequence I want my Palace to be a very happy place.'

He had visited quite a number of different States since his reign in Vienz began and he thought that in the majority of them the Royal families were extremely dull.

Even if the Queen or Princess appeared to be fond of her husband, he was generally bored with her and he made it clear that she was not expected to take part in any intelligent conversations.

Watching them the Prince had sworn to himself that was a life he would find intolerable.

'What I wish for is that my wife should be in love with me and I with her,' he determined.

He told himself that so far his heart had not been really touched despite the often fiery passion of his love-making, and he was intelligent enough to realise that for him an *affaire-de-coeur* was just a passing pleasure.

The love he was seeking would last for the rest of his life.

Perhaps he was hoping for the impossible.

Maybe it was something he would never find.

Yet the books which filled his library and which he pored over when he had time told him it was possible.

There were many examples in history of a love that had made a man greater because of it.

How, he now reflected, could an arranged marriage, which simply enhanced the status of a country, really be satisfying?

Every man wanted to find the true and perfect love that had been sought since the beginning of civilisation.

'Can I fall in love with this young girl?' he asked.

A Power greater than himself gave him the answer.

'Only if I do, however much I am then pushed and shoved by those who think they know better than I do, will I ask her to marry me.'

This decision was ringing in his ears as he walked out at the back of the Palace. Then he stood for a moment gazing at the beauty all around him.

The gardens blazed with blossom of every colour and beyond them was the artificial lake his father had made and which he had improved considerably.

It was perfectly cemented and attractively designed and in the centre of it was a group of cupids surrounding a fine statue of the Goddess Aphrodite.

He had been very young when he had learnt about the Goddess of Love.

His teacher told him all about Delphi and the Gods of Olympus and the story of Aphrodite excited him.

He had found pictures of her in books and when he was older he had visited Greece to see her. He had learnt from the Greeks how much they revered and loved her.

The flowers that bordered the lake and the trees he had planted were always a delight to him and he felt that no one could fail to be moved by the beauty he was now surveying.

There was no sign of the Princess or the Comte.

Then he realised they would probably be sitting in the comfortable pavilion he had built in the form of a small Temple looking out at the glorious statue of Aphrodite in the centre of the lake.

It was where he often sat himself and his mother had always gone there when she wanted to pray rather than go to the private Chapel in the Palace.

Slowly the Prince walked towards the little Temple which shone white against the green of the trees.

He thought as he went that one day he would take the woman he loved and who loved him to Greece and they would move from Temple to Temple looking for Aphrodite because she had already blessed them.

She had always meant so much to him personally that he had never had an *affaire-de-coeur* in Greece.

He knew the reason even though he did not always put it into words. He was waiting for the day when he would introduce the woman he really loved to the Goddess from whom their love came.

He had often told himself he was being ridiculously sentimental, but he could not fight against everything he had believed in ever since he had first thought of women as desirable.

To enjoy a better view of Aphrodite he did not walk along the side of the lake but through the tall trees and he reached the Temple from the rear.

As he did so and was just about to walk round and tell them he was there, he heard the Comte saying,

"My darling, my sweet. It is wonderful to be alone with you for this beautiful moment, but it will be agony when we have to go back to the Palace."

The Prince froze.

Then a soft voice replied,

"I love you, Ruta, and so how can I possibly accept Prince Nicolo as Papa and everyone else wants me to do?"

"You will have to do it because it will help both your country and ours," the Comte answered. "But when you marry the Prince, I will have to go away."

"No! *No!*"

The Princess's words were a cry from her heart.

"How *could* you leave me? How could I possibly endure being here if I could not even see you?"

"Have you thought what agony it will be for me?" the Comte asked.

"It will be far worse for me if I cannot see you. I would rather die than lose you, Ruta."

"You must not talk like that, my darling, it is wrong of me to listen to you, yet as you know I have loved you since the moment I first set eyes on you."

"And I love you. You were the man of my dreams and since I met you I have dreamt every night that we might be together. Oh, Ruta, darling, please marry me so that I can be with you for ever."

He tried to laugh, but it was only a whimper.

"Do you think for one moment your father would accept me? He is determined that you should make a grand marriage and what could be more splendid than being the wife of Prince Nicolo of Vienz?"

"I don't want to be grand. I don't want to be the wife of a Ruling Prince. I want to be *your* wife and to be with you, Ruta."

The Comte groaned.

"God knows I want nothing else, but I tell you, my darling, it is impossible."

He then obviously looked at his watch as he said,

"Now we must go back to the Palace. The Prince will be returning from his ride and you must make yourself charming to him."

"Oh, what am I to say, what am I to do?" Princess Marziale wailed. "I have no wish to talk to him. It is just agony when I cannot be with you."

"I feel the same," said the Comte. "But we must do our duty. As you know I owe my allegiance to Vienz."

"Then kiss me. Kiss me before we must go back," the Princess sighed.

Listening, as if he had been turned into stone, the Prince was now aware that they were on their feet.

The Princess was in the Comte's arms.

Very cautiously he stepped away from the Temple, being careful that he did not make a sound as he moved through the undergrowth.

Then he saw them walking slowly along the side of the lake.

They were not speaking, they were not touching each other, but he knew after what he had just heard that their hearts were beating in unison.

Their love was an agony within their breasts and at the same time a rapture beyond words.

The Prince waited until they had reached the end of the lake and were moving up the lawn towards the Palace, and then he went into the Temple and sat down on the very comfortable sofa they had just vacated.

He looked across at Aphrodite in the centre of the lake with the cupids playing round her.

Then he asked her, as if she was a real person and indeed she was very real to him,

"What can I do? What the hell can I do?"

He sat there for a long time.

Then, feeling that the Goddess Aphrodite had not answered him, he slipped out of the Temple.

He walked slowly back through the woods and no one watching for him from the Palace would guess that he had been down at the lake – least of all the couple who had just come from there.

He entered the Palace by another door and found two of his *aides-de-camp* were waiting for him.

They exclaimed,

"Oh, there you are, Sire! We have been wondering where Your Royal Highness could be and the Princess has been asking for you."

"I am sorry about that," the Prince replied. "But I had something I needed to do."

He went into his office and sat down at the desk.

"There are a number of people waiting to see Your Royal Highness," an *aide-de-camp* said, "including the Prime Minister."

"Tell them I am far too busy to see anyone at the moment. If they really want to see me and it is urgent, tell them to come back again this afternoon."

"You will not see them before the gala luncheon, Sire?"

"No, I want to be left alone for the moment."

The *aide-de-camp* hurried from the room and then the Prince sat back in his chair.

He knew now he had to escape from the impossible position he found himself in.

He must also save Princess Marziale from breaking her heart and the heart of Comte Ruta.

For a time he could not think how he could do it.

Then he thought that the one thing he would like to be was an ordinary man and to be able to seek love as any man could do if he was not weighed down by a Crown.

It was a shackle he could not escape from and as long as he had to wear it, he had no chance of finding love, the love that others found because they were not hamstrung by their own position in life.

He sat for some time just staring with sightless eyes at the window in front of him.

Outside the sun was shining, but it seemed to him as if a darkness was gradually encroaching upon him.

'I *have* to be free,' he determined.

Then, almost as if a strange voice was telling him and perhaps the voice came from Aphrodite herself, he knew what he must do.

He picked up a pen and wrote quickly and without a pause on the thick engraved writing paper in front of him on the desk.

Then he placed it in an envelope and addressed it.

Putting it into his pocket he walked out of the room to find an *aide-de-camp* waiting for him to appear.

The Prince walked past him to the stairs that led to his private apartments. He went straight into his bedroom and found his valet was waiting for him to change after his ride.

"I hears Your Royal Highness was back," the valet said, "and I expected you'd want to change afore you went down the garden."

"I will change now, Texxo," the Prince replied and then he changed his mind. "No, I want to send a message downstairs to say I don't feel well and will not be down for luncheon. Then come back as I have something special for you to do."

Texxo, who had been with the Prince ever since he left school, now looked at him in surprise.

"Your Royal Highness not goin' to the luncheon!" he exclaimed. "But I understands it's a special party for Her Royal Highness and the Prime Minister be comin'."

"Do as you are told, Texxo," the Prince scolded him sharply.

The valet hurried from the room and then the Prince walked to the window to stand looking out at the garden.

When Texxo came back, he turned round.

"There be a right old flutter downstairs, Your Royal Highness," said Texxo. "The Lord Chamberlain wants to know if you'd like him to send for a doctor."

"When I want a doctor, I will send for one. Now Texxo, you know I have trusted you since you first looked after me – I think I was about sixteen at the time."

Texxo who was getting on for forty smiled.

"It were nearly eighteen year ago and Your Royal Highness has changed a bit since then."

"I am going to change a good deal more now, and you will be the only person who knows what I am going to do until I am too far away for them to interfere."

"What be you be goin' to do, if I may ask?"

"I am going to be an ordinary man for a short time and I want you now to help me go away from the Palace without anyone being aware of where we are going."

"Am I comin' with Your Royal Highness?"

"Yes, at least as far as Venice. I am not quite sure where I will be going after that."

"What'll they do here?" Texxo asked nervously.

"If they follow my orders, they will do nothing."

The Prince drew from his pocket the letter he had written and put it on his dressing table.

"They will find this when I have gone. But I want you, Texxo, to help me disappear without anyone having the slightest idea of what is happening."

His voice deepened as he continued,

"We will have to be very very careful. Otherwise, as you know, I will be stopped before I am even free of the Palace let alone the frontier."

"Well, I don't blame Your Royal Highness," Texxo remarked. "Equally there'll be a real hullabaloo when they discovers you've gone!"

"I want you to tell them I have a splitting headache and I am not to be disturbed under any circumstances until I feel better. Say I know what it is and what has caused it and that I have no wish to see a doctor.

"You will pack just enough for us to take on the horses we shall be riding. Order one horse for yourself and one for another servant. Tell them you have a special letter to deliver for me and no one will be interested as to who you are taking with you."

Quite unexpectedly Texxo laughed.

"It'll be like old times, when Your Royal Highness was a young boy and you used to ask me to let you out of the side door and tell no one where you'd gone."

The Prince laughed too.

"I remember that. It was because I wanted to play with children my parents did not think were smart enough for me. Thanks to you, I enjoyed every moment I spent with them!"

"And whose children will Your Royal Highness be meetin' now?" Texxo asked cheekily.

"That is exactly what I don't know. I just want to fly away from all this attention I am receiving and have a chance to be an ordinary person. A man like yourself, who can do just what he wants without people interfering and without being protected at every turn – "

His voice became sarcastic as he added,

"Not from an enemy so much as from the people who claw at me because they desire something."

"That be true enough and I don't blame Your Royal Highness. But, as I've already said, there'll be a hell of a fuss about this. I only hopes I don't lose my head or find myself behind bars."

"You know they will never touch you, Texxo, when you belong to me."

"That's all right as long as you're here, but it's not so funny when you ain't."

"I tell you what, you will stay away too and wait for me to come back with you before I return home."

"Now that be talkin' sense. Your Royal Highness must understand that if they thinks I had helped you run away they'll force me one way or another to tell 'em where you be."

"Very well! As I have said, you can come with me and when I return, if I do return, I will pick you up so that we come back together."

"What's Your Royal Highness told 'em downstairs in that letter?" Texxo asked, pointing with his thumb.

"I have told them I have a special mission which is important and which will affect this country particularly. I therefore trust them to keep it a secret that I am not in the Palace. If the public ask questions, they are to be told that I am just suffering from a bad attack of influenza."

"What about them doctors?"

"I have said that they are to say I am being looked after and I hope soon to be restored to perfect health."

Texxo laughed as if he could not help it.

"All I can say now is that Your Royal Highness has always been different from any of them others, and as you knows I've much admired you for it. But this certainly be somethin' we've never tried before."

"We are going to try it now and if we fail, we fail. When we come back I expect them to applaud my decision when they have learnt why I made it."

There was a small inflection in the Prince's voice that told Texxo, who knew him so well, he was not certain that he would be successful.

Because he loved the Prince as he had ever since he had looked after him as a boy, Texxo added,

"I've never known Your Royal Highness not get your own way on everythin' sooner or later. If that's what you be determined to have, it'll be what you want and I'll bet my last penny on it."

"Thank you, Texxo, that is just what I want to hear. Now start the packing and I only want the simple ordinary clothes that a man in the street would wear. I will also want plenty of ready money."

"That'll not be difficult. I've often thought it were a mistake to keep too much in the safe in this here room. But as usual you're right, and now we wants it, it's there!"

"Thank goodness for that," the Prince sighed.

"There's one more thing I has to ask Your Royal Highness. How long do you think we'll be away?"

"I have no idea, Texxo. I suppose until I find what I am seeking or come crawling back and admit I have failed."

"That is something I've never known you admit yet and I hopes I never hears Your Royal Highness mention it in the future."

He went out of the room as he spoke and the Prince laughed.

He had learnt of old that Texxo always had the last word.

CHAPTER TWO

The Palace was concentrating on the gala luncheon being given that day in honour of the Princess Marziale.

So no one heard the Prince and Texxo slip quietly down the backstairs.

Texxo had already been to the stables and ordered two of the best horses to be saddled. He told the grooms that they were for an extra special journey that had to be undertaken as soon as luncheon was finished.

The grooms, if they thought at all, assumed it was something to do with the Princess Marziale – doubtless an announcement of the marriage between her and the Prince.

Taking the horses from them, Texxo tied them up in a quiet part of the garden where no one was likely to go until the festivities were over.

Then he went back to find the Prince had already dressed in his ordinary clothes and was sitting at the desk in his bedroom.

"Has Your Royal Highness told them in the Palace where we'll be goin'?" asked Texxo.

The Prince knew he was joking.

"No, for the simple reason I don't know myself. What I have done, and you might just as well know all my secrets, is to give instructions that because of his excellent services in escorting here such a charming guest as the

Princess Marziale, the Comte Ruta is to be made a Duke of Vienz. It is in my power to do so."

Texxo looked surprised but he did not say anything.

The Prince was smiling quietly to himself as he was thinking that the Princess's father would not be so adverse to his daughter marrying a Duke if she was unable to catch a reigning Prince.

Then they left his bedroom and concentrated on moving swiftly and silently out of the Palace.

Texxo was carrying their clothes packed into hardy saddlebags which soldiers used when they went on long journeys on horseback.

The Prince smiled as he saw that as usual Texxo had thought of everything.

On his return from the stables, he had brought up something for the Prince to eat when he passed through the kitchen.

It was certainly not the excellent fare they were enjoying in the banqueting hall, but it was a piece of *foie gras* of which His Royal Highness was particularly fond – and there was toast and butter to eat with it.

Fortunately there was champagne in the cupboard of the Prince's sitting room.

As Texxo had poured him out a glass, the Prince suggested,

"Have a glass yourself, and drink to our success on this adventure which could dramatically change the rest of my life."

"I'll drink Your Royal Highness's health," Texxo replied. "But at thi very moment I *am* worryin' about your future."

"Well, stop worrying and let's get on!"

He had eaten the pâté and now he finished his glass of champagne and went to the door.

"You have everything, Texxo?" he asked.

"I hope so. Your Royal Highness hasn't forgotten the money?"

The Prince put his hand to his head.

"Fool that I am!" he exclaimed. "Actually I have, because I always have an equerry carrying any money I need."

"Well, now Your Royal Highness has to be your own equerry, you'll have to be careful about that sort of thing!"

The Prince laughed and went to the safe which was in his sitting room.

It had a special lock which only he could work and he was delighted to see the large amount of money stashed inside the safe.

He had deliberately always asked for more than he needed when he required money to buy gifts or anything for himself.

This was because when he wanted money he had to ask for it as if he was nothing more than a schoolboy. It was a strange regulation that had been passed down from one Ruler to another.

The Rulers had their money kept in the State bank and not in the Palace and this the Prince found extremely tiresome.

If he needed money he had to send an *aide-de-camp* to the Keeper of the Privy Purse, who then had to be in touch with the Chancellor of the Exchequer. Eventually hours later the Prince received the money he required.

Not because he wished to conceal his finances but because it irritated him, the Prince had over the years put away a fairly considerable sum in his private safe.

Now he was able to take out a great deal more than he was likely to need on this escapade.

'I will have to come back some time,' he said to himself, 'win or lose.'

They rode away keeping to the trees until they were outside the Palace grounds.

As they did so, the Prince told himself that if the Goddess of Love was keeping watch over him he would not come back a failure.

*

It was a lovely day and the sun was shining.

By the time the Prince reined in his horse they were on the borders of Vienz and crossing into Italy.

It was always quite impossible to guard every inch of any frontier and, although Vienz boasted a large Army, the frontier forts were several miles apart and it was easy enough to avoid them.

The Prince, in fact, had visited every fort in the last few months and he noted that they were strong enough to repel an enemy. They were also pleasant enough to make the men who manned them enjoy being posted to one.

He had built up his Army very carefully ever since he succeeded his father.

He was well aware that many small countries as well as large ones like Great Britain had, after the defeat of Napoleon, thought it unlikely there would ever be a great European war again.

He had been particularly astonished that the British, who were now busily creating an enormous Empire, should believe this and they had not, in his opinion, taken enough trouble over their Army.

He had visited England before his father died and he had thought then that the soldiers were badly fed and not enough attention was given to their training.

However there were exceptions to this as a number of aristocrats, like Lord Cardigan, raised their own private Army and paid for it out of their own purse.

The Prince had considered this idea for some time and then he decided that it would be inadvisable in his own small country.

There was always the likelihood that the owner of a private Army might have ambitious ideas of his own and he could use it to depose the Ruler and take over the throne for himself.

But the Prince did appreciate that Lord Cardigan's Army was dressed more smartly than other Regiments, especially those in attendance on Her Majesty the Queen.

"Now we're in Italy," Texxo piped up, "where be Your Royal Highness aimin' for?"

"We are now going to Venice, and if we go a little further before we stop for the night, we should be there by midday tomorrow."

Texxo did not reply, but the Prince knew that he was enjoying himself.

The horses they were riding were not tired. Texxo had been sensible enough to choose not only the youngest of the trained horses in the stables but also those that were best bred.

The stallion the Prince was riding was one of his favourites and he knew that he would carry him for days without showing the least sign of fatigue.

He was thinking of the horses when they stopped for the night.

It was in a small village where there was an inn that appeared to be clean with a large stable attached.

When they asked if they could stay the night, the publican was delighted to accommodate them, and it was obvious that, situated in a rather barren part of the land, he did not often have visitors.

The Prince saw that their horses were provided with fresh straw and the most expensive oats available.

Then he and Texxo walked into the inn.

It was a small place with a limited choice of wine, but there was a table where visitors could sit in reasonable comfort.

The food when it came was more or less edible and upstairs the rooms were without carpets and the beds were hard but they were clean.

As Texxo hung up the clothes the Prince had taken off, he remarked,

"I'm wonderin' what they'll be sayin' at the Palace when they finds Your Royal Highness ain't there."

"I made it clear in the letter I wrote," the Prince replied, "that I was going on a very difficult and secret mission. No one outside the Palace is to know that I was not suffering from the illness that explained my absence at the gala luncheon."

"They'll be in a real flap all right. Whatever Your Royal Highness has told 'em, they'll find it hard not to send a search party after you."

"I don't think they will be stupid enough to do so," the Prince said, "and if they do, we must be quite certain they don't find me. Now go off to bed and stop worrying. And do remember you don't address me as 'Your Royal Highness'."

"It just slips out," admitted Texxo.

"Well, control it. If I have to go back without even a chance of achieving what I am setting out to do, I will never forgive you."

"I'll be very careful," Texxo promised. "But after so many years it comes natural like."

He pulled down the blind as there were no curtains at the window for him to close.

"Now what time shall I call Your – I means *you*?"

"About six o'clock, Texxo. We have a long way to go, but I am determined to reach Venice tomorrow."

"We'll do it," Texxo called cheerily as he opened the door. "Goodnight and may God bless you, no one knows better than He do how much you're needed in Vienz."

He did not wait for the Prince to answer, but closed the door and went into the next room.

The Prince laughed to himself.

He reflected, as he had often done before, that he would rather be with Texxo on a special operation than with anyone else.

He knew if he had taken one of his equerries with him, he would have been asking questions.

Why was he leaving?

Where was he going?

What was he planning?

How soon would they be going back?

They were questions to which at the moment he had no answers.

He closed his eyes and was ready to go to sleep and then he was ruminating again that Aphrodite was watching over him.

He felt sure that the great Goddess would not let him down.

*

They had a well-cooked breakfast before they left and the publican was delighted with the money the Prince gave him.

"It's not often we has gentlemen like you to stay," he said, "and me wife were sayin' so to me last night, if you and your kind be likely to come here again we'll put curtains at the windows and carpets on the floor."

"I was very comfortable," the Prince replied, "and tell your wife I appreciate how clean the room was and the bed."

"I'll tell her and we'll be a-hopin' we'll see you another time."

"I hope so too," the Prince added, as he shook the man by the hand.

Then he mounted his stallion, which was only too eager to ride off at a sharp pace and broke into a gallop as soon as they were clear of the village.

It was much later that the Prince saw with relief that they were nearing Venice.

He had visited Venice several times and he thought of it an entrancing, unique and beautiful city with a special atmosphere all of its own.

He loved the ancient Palaces and the canals and the magnificent Piazza San Marco.

Apart from all its heritage and history there was something remarkable about the air of Venice. It seemed to contain a magic he had never found in any other City.

Because his father had been very broad-minded, the Prince had visited a great number of Cities in Europe, but never in any of them had he found quite the enchantment of Venice.

He had always thought that, if he was forced to live outside his own country, he would stay in Venice.

He would be content just savouring the beauty of it all and he had sometimes thought that perhaps what he found in Venice was what he was looking for in a woman.

He could not put it into words, yet it was something so perfect and different that one could not compare it with anywhere else in the world.

Now as they approached Venice the sun was still shining and the lagoon seemed to reflect the light from the sky.

His first glimpse of the lagoon told the Prince that it was very much a part of what he was seeking.

The first priority was to stable the horses and it was important they should be well looked after if he and Texxo were to wander around the City.

The Prince knew that there was an excellent hotel on the outskirts of Venice. It was where he had left his horses before and found that they were well cared for there.

"It is a long time," he confided to Texxo, "since I have been to the *Hotel Rialto*. So they are not likely to recognise me. You must tell them that you want them to look after the horses on behalf of the Prince of Vienz who will be coming to stay in the hotel in perhaps two or three weeks time."

Texxo knew exactly what was required and so he went ahead of the Prince and spoke to the man in charge of the stables and he was suitably impressed by the reference to the Prince.

He showed first Texxo and then the Prince some excellent stalls. There was not only light and air, but they were also wide enough for the horses to be comfortable when they lay down.

They put their horses into their stalls and as they did so the Prince decided what he would do next.

He wanted to enjoy the beauty of Venice and to see it alone.

When they left the stables, he found a seat in the garden and sat down on it.

"What I want you to do, Texxo," he said, "is to go inside and book two ordinary bedrooms. Tell them as you did in the stables that we expect Prince Nicolo of Vienz to be joining us soon.

"In the meantime you and I have business to do in Venice. You don't have to say what it is, but simply it is exceedingly important and you are obeying the orders of His Royal Highness."

"That won't be difficult," Texxo smiled.

"Of course you will need some money and it would be wise for me to give you a considerable amount – just in case I am assaulted by a mugger or have it stolen from me by a pickpocket without my even knowing about it."

"You'd be too sharp by this time to be as foolish as that," Texxo replied.

"It has happened to better men than me, but I am prepared."

He showed Texxo that he had an envelope in his belt and he then handed him a large handful of notes.

Texxo put them away carefully in the inside pocket of his coat.

"I will join you at dinner," the Prince said, "but if I am late or don't come, please don't worry about me as I am looking for adventure and, who knows, I may well find it today!"

"Well, you take care of yourself. I've no wish to take a riderless horse back to the Palace and say I lost you on the way. It's somethin' they won't think funny."

The Prince laughed.

"Nor will I, Texxo. I promise I will take good care of myself, but I want to have a good look round and you know I have always loved Venice."

Texxo did not answer.

He handed the Prince the saddlebag with his clothes which he had been carrying with his own bag since they left the stables.

He sat in the garden while the Prince went down to the water's edge.

There were gondolas for hire for those staying in the hotel and, as there were quite a number of gondolas to choose from, it was obvious the hotel was not full.

The Prince thought with satisfaction that it would mean it would be easy to move about on the canals and it would spoil it if he encountered crowds of holidaymakers.

He told the man in charge that he was staying at the hotel and his horses were in the stable – his friend who was accompanying him was looking them for him.

He added that he also wanted the best gondola for himself and tipped the man generously as he spoke.

He was therefore provided with a gondola which he expected was kept for the most important guests.

Then putting his saddlebag into the gondola and feeling the excitement of a young boy, he set off down the canal.

He had always enjoyed manipulating a gondola and he was as adept at it, he considered, as any of the men who made their living by propelling one around the City.

He found the Piazzetta and deliberately moved into the small narrow canals opening off it. He had found them entrancing on his first visit to Venice when he was only sixteen.

Then back into the Grand Canal for a glance at the Ca' d'Oro – the House of Gold – which had enchanted him at an early age.

He had told himself that one day he would live in a house which would bear the same name and he had then thought it would be amusing to imitate it by painting the front of his Palace in gold. But his mother had persuaded him it would be too ostentatious and he had therefore given up the idea when he came to the throne.

The Prince steered the gondola further down the Grand Canal and then turned into one of the side canals.

There were great houses rising from the waters on one side and on the other side less fashionable houses with a yard in front and on these grew bushes and flowers.

There was no other gondola on this canal and the Prince stopped to admire the flowers.

Flowers were always a part of Venetian life even though there were no gardens like his at the Palace.

Then he decided he would move on.

As he did so, he was suddenly aware that at a large house just ahead of him that overhung the water there was someone at one of the windows on the second floor.

It was a woman.

She appeared to be leaning out of it dangerously.

He thought that she must have dropped something into the water below and so she was peering out in the hope of spotting it.

Then to his utter astonishment he saw that she was climbing out of the window.

She was holding tightly onto a rope that appeared to be fastened to something inside the house.

She then swung herself free from the window and the Prince could see that she was sliding down towards the water beneath her.

With a swift movement he moved the gondola so that it slid underneath her just before her feet touched the water.

As she collapsed into the gondola, she looked up at him and at the same time she flung the rope free from her.

41

"*Quickly*! Quickly!" she cried. "Take me away before they find I have gone!"

She was agitated and bordering on the hysterical.

The Prince noticed that she was Italian and a lady. She was certainly not, as it had occurred to him when she was first descending, a thief.

Because of the urgency in her voice he accelerated the movement of the gondola.

They shot up the canal as fast as he could propel it at a considerable speed.

When they were almost out of sight of the house she had descended from, the Prince asked her,

"Where do you want to go?"

"Anywhere as long as it is away from here and they cannot find me," she replied anxiously.

She swept back her hair that had fallen over her face when she was descending from the window.

The Prince noticed at once that she was both very young and very beautiful.

In fact unusually so.

Her face was small and her features perfect.

Her eyes were large and he could see that there was an expression of fear in them.

He thought at first she was little more than a child, yet when she moved he could see the outline of her breasts.

She was certainly young – but a woman.

She seated herself more comfortably on the floor of the gondola and she was looking back apprehensively at the house she had come from.

Only when it was completely out of sight and the Prince had asked her again where she wanted to go, did she look at him.

He knew she realised that he was not as she would have anticipated an ordinary gondolier.

"I am afraid," she mumbled nervously, "that this is a – private gondola and not for hire as I thought at first."

"Shall I say I am delighted to be of service," the Prince said. "But you must tell me where you want to go."

"Away from Venice as quickly as possible, but if that is asking too much of you, please drop me on the other side of the Grand Canal."

She drew in her breath and continued,

"I will find a gondola to take me across the lagoon to the mainland where I can disappear – "

"Have you any idea exactly where you wish to go?" the Prince asked her again.

"Just any place I can hide until I decide where to go next."

"Is it too much to ask why you are running away."

"I am running away because I am frightened, more frightened than I have ever been in my whole life!"

The Prince was now propelling the gondola more slowly and carefully towards the Grand Canal.

"Of course," he said, "I am curious as to why you have run away. But you must have somewhere to go and enough money to take you there."

The girl looked at him and gave a little scream.

"I did not think of money," she cried. "Of course I must pay my way, but, as I have always had someone to look after me and pay for what I needed, I never thought of it until now."

"It seems to me that you are making a big mistake," the Prince remarked, "in racing off into the unknown and with an empty pocket."

"I have to do it, there is nothing else I can do. I thought if I fell into the canal and drowned, it would be easier than staying where I was!"

She gave a little sigh before she added,

"But as I can swim I expect when I was actually in the water I would have found it very difficult not to save myself."

"Of course you would have done and as the most precious possession we have is life, it would be very silly to throw it all away in a dirty canal."

"There was nothing else I could do. It was just by chance that you were there."

"I hope one day you will think it a lucky chance, and I think that for the moment you are safe enough from anyone who is looking for you and you can tell me who you are and why you have run away."

"My name is Sacia," she answered.

There was a pause and the Prince guessed that she was thinking it would be a mistake to tell him any more.

"My name is Nico," he told her.

Sacia smiled.

"I am certain they christened you Nicolo, which is a very popular name in Italy, but I am sure that you like to shorten it because it's easier to say."

"That is a clever deduction of yours. Now, Sacia, I am waiting for you to tell me why you are doing anything so incredibly foolish as to try to kill yourself."

"I was really just trying to escape – and there was no other way as they had – locked me in my bedroom."

"Who did?" the Prince asked her automatically and then realised that he should not have done.

"I am not being inquisitive," he said, "so no names, but just tell me what you are hiding from."

"A man they want me to marry."

The Prince thought it was an answer he might have expected.

Only fate or his beloved Goddess Aphrodite could have brought him someone who was in the same situation as he was in himself.

"Tell me more," he begged Sacia.

"It cannot be interesting to you when you are just a stranger and I think first I should say thank you for being so kind as to rescue me and take me away at once."

She paused as if thinking it over, then went on,

"Actually I don't think they will find out for the next hour or so that I am not in my room."

"What will happen then?" the Prince enquired.

"The man they want me to marry is arriving soon and I was told I was to accept him when he proposed to me. As you already realise, I would rather die than marry him!"

45

"What is wrong with him?"

"He is old, he is repulsive and I know he is cruel to those who serve him."

The Prince raised his eyebrows.

"He has been married twice already and both his wives have died in somewhat mysterious circumstances. I am really sure in my own mind that he poisoned them or disposed of them in some other dastardly way because he was tired of them as they did not please him."

"I am finding this very hard to believe, Sacia. How could anyone be so cruel to anyone as pretty as you?"

"Women don't stay pretty for ever," Sacia replied, as if he had asked a serious question. "They grow ill or old and perhaps they don't produce as many children as their husband wants. I think it may be the reason why the man I am telling you about rid himself of his last two wives."

She gave a little sigh before she added,

"It may not have been their fault that there was not the heir he desired."

"So he has chosen you as his third wife?"

"If you saw him, you would understand why I ran away."

"But you did not run! It was very brave of you to lower yourself out of the window."

"I was so frightened I just had to escape somehow."

"What do you intend to do now?" the Prince asked.

"It was so stupid of me to come away without any money. I was in such a hurry I did not think of anything but not being there when he arrived."

"Surely you have friends who will look after you and help you?"

There was a brief silence and then Sacia replied,

"I cannot think of anyone who would not be scared of Papa and who would not tell him where I was hiding."

The Prince reflected it was obvious that her father was someone of consequence – and indeed so was the man he wanted her to marry.

It all seemed so extraordinary that he himself was in the same predicament.

He thought that anyone he knew would tell him he should take the girl back to where she would be safe with her family.

As if she could read his thoughts, Sacia asked,

"Are you now thinking that you should do the right thing and take me back to where you found me?"

"It might be correct, but I promise I will do what you ask of me as long as it is within my power."

"The trouble is, Nico, I am not at all certain *what* I can do. There is a friend who might be kind to me, but she lives in Paris and I have no money to go there. Although I know that she was rather impressed by Papa."

"Surely there must be a servant you can trust? An old Nanny or someone like that."

"My Nanny died two years ago," Sacia answered, "and the servants in the Palazzo are all too afraid of Papa to do anything to displease him."

The Prince noticed that she said '*the Palazzo*'.

He knew that quite a number of the grand houses in Venice were called 'Palaces'. Also hotels were sometimes named in the same way, but it did not necessarily imply a Royal residence as in other countries.

By this time they were reaching the top end of the Grand Canal furthest from San Marco.

"Now where do you wish to go?" the Prince asked. "Personally I think they would be more likely to look for you on a small uninhabited island than they would outside Venice."

"Of course you are right. I never thought of that. But how can I go there without any money."

"I will take you, Sacia, and if you have time to think over what you can do, you will perhaps remember someone who could help you or somewhere you can stay until your father changes his mind about your marriage. But that may take longer than we think."

"If I know anything, Papa will take months if not years to recover from the way I have behaved. He will never change his mind about my marriage."

"Then what will you do?" the Prince asked her.

"I will have to find some way of working for my living. It is something I have never done of course. But I can cook and sew very well and I speak quite a number of languages."

As she spoke the last word she gave a little cry,

"Of course, I must be a teacher. People want to learn languages and will pay me to teach their children."

The Prince smiled.

"You look little more than a child yourself."

"I am nearly nineteen. That is one reason why Papa is anxious for me to marry."

"Is this the first proposal you have had?"

"No, I have had two others. But Papa did not think them good enough for me and sent the men away. If I have to marry someone, I would rather marry any of them than the man he wants to be my husband."

As she spoke the fear and horror was back in her voice and he knew the prospect was still terrifying her.

"Please trust me," he said, "and I will tell you what we will do."

Sacia gave a little murmur but did not interrupt.

"I will take you at once to where I have my horses. We can immediately ride away from Venice before the hue and cry is organised to some place which is safe. That is to say if you can ride."

"Of course I can," replied Sacia. "Will you really do this for me? How can you be so kind and so different from other people when you have never even seen me until I fell into your gondola?"

"I can understand why you are running away," the Prince added, "because actually I myself am running away too, but I will not bother you with the details now. I am sure together we can find a solution to your problem and perhaps to mine as well."

He felt not very optimistic as he spoke, but it was a really strange coincidence that they should both be in the same position.

Their Guardian Angels, if it was indeed they who had brought them together, would he hoped find a solution, one which so far he, at any rate, had overlooked.

"You are so kind, so unbelievably kind," Sacia was saying. "I can only say a special prayer of thankfulness tonight that you have been sent to save me when I least expected it."

"Do you think that by now," the Prince asked, "they will be out scouring Venice for you?"

He saw Sacia shudder as she answered,

"Not quite yet, but *he* will soon arrive and they will send upstairs for me."

"All they will find is your rope dangling outside the window and if you are not in the water below, there will undoubtedly be a hue and cry to find you."

Sacia made a little sound which was like a bird or a small animal being hunted.

"Once it is known that I am missing, there are many people in Venice who will recognise me."

"In which case, Sacia, if we hurry, we will just have time to pick up my horses and ride across to the mainland before the search begins."

They very quickly reached the *Hotel Rialto*.

While the horses were saddled up and his saddlebag attached, the Prince told Texxo briefly what had happened and instructed him to return the gondola to its owner.

He reckoned they would still have time to ride over the causeway to the mainland before the search began.

This they safely managed, after he had instructed Texxo to stay at the hotel and await his further orders.

They then galloped across country westwards for an hour or so.

There were trees in the far distance, but none near them and they moved on rather more rapidly.

*

After a while the Prince saw ahead what appeared to be a small village.

Already the sun was sinking rapidly and darkness would soon follow and they rode on faster towards the few houses he could see ahead.

There were a number of cottages and beyond them a larger house and the Prince thought it might be a place where they could stay.

"Are we stopping here?" Sacia asked nervously.

"It will soon be dark," replied the Prince, "and we must find somewhere to stay the night. Then we will leave early in the morning before anyone is up."

"I feel I am a terrible nuisance to you, Nico. But if you were not here and I was on my own, I am sure they would find me and drag me back."

"Which is the one eventuality we intend to avoid – so come on, Sacia."

They rode towards the larger house.

As they reached it and dismounted, he realised she was taller than he had thought but still quite small.

Sacia's dress was very expensive looking and her long auburn hair that had fallen over her shoulders when she had climbed down the rope made her look young and innocent.

The Prince took off his riding coat.

"Put this round your shoulders," he said, "as if you are feeling the cold. It will hide the fact that your dress must have cost quite a lot of money, which any woman would notice."

"I had not thought of that," Sacia murmured.

"I think too you should put this handkerchief of mine over your hair. It will make you look more ordinary and I will explain we stayed out later than we intended. Incidentally I think I should say you are my sister and we must choose a name for us."

Sacia laughed.

"I feel sure this is not happening and – we are just dreaming it."

"Well, unless your story is completely untrue, it is all happening now and it is so important that what we say is believed. We must not make anyone suspicious."

"No, of course not, you are so right and so clever," Sacia sighed.

"Then what shall we call ourselves?" he persisted. "It's vital that it does not sound a grand name."

He picked up his bag and they were both silent for a moment as they led their horses towards the larger house.

"My Nanny, who I mentioned just now, was called Noemi. Will that do for a name?"

"Excellent! And because you speak like a lady, I think you should say as little as possible and let me do the talking."

"I was going to anyway. You are so kind and I am so lucky to have found you. I will not trust myself to do anything unless you tell me what to do."

"That is just the right attitude that every woman should take!" the Prince remarked sardonically.

He thought as he was speaking that it was the sort of light-hearted remark that he would have made in Paris or among his own friends to raise a laugh.

To his surprise Sacia responded,

"That is exactly what all men think and if a woman is intelligent she does not argue about it."

The Prince wanted to reply, but they had by now reached the house.

It turned out to be a rather poor-class bar at which two middle-aged men, obviously workmen, were drinking and a publican in shirtsleeves was serving them.

The Prince then walked up to the bar and spoke in a deliberately rather coarse Italian,

"I wonder if you can help me. My sister and I have had a little trouble with our horses. As it is getting late, is it possible we can stay the night and leave early in the morning? Can you let us have two bedrooms?"

The publican looked them up and down.

It was as if he was calculating if they could afford it and then he answered,

"I've two empty rooms, but they're not very smart, and you looks to me as if you wants one of them grand hotels which be springin' up round here everywhere."

"We will be extremely happy if you could make us comfortable in your two rooms," the Prince answered. "My sister is very tired and so am I. We have done enough riding for one day."

One of the men at the bar laughed.

"That's what they all say," he blurted out.

"In this case it just happens to be true," parried the Prince.

"Just you wait here," the publican came in, "while I goes and talks to the Missus. I'm sure she'll put you up somehow, but it'll cost you – "

"I am quite willing to pay and if you would like it in advance, I will give it to you now."

"No, no," the man said, "of course I trust you," and then he hurried away.

Next the Prince suggested,

"As I could do with a drink myself, let me stand you men one too. I assure you I am grateful to be able to rest here."

"If you've been ridin' for long, it's ain't surprisin' you're tired," one of the men remarked.

"My sister wanted to see Venice and now we have seen it and there is indeed plenty to see."

The men thought this was a joke and they were laughing as the publican returned.

"The Missus says she'll have two rooms ready for you in a short while. She supposes you'll want somethin' to eat."

"We are very grateful that she should have thought of it. And these two gentlemen would like to join me in thanking you with a glass of your best wine."

"What about the little lady?" the publican enquired.

Sacia had sat down in a rickety chair with a small table beside it – quite a number of glasses of wine must have been spilt on it at one time or another.

The Prince walked across to her.

"What would you like to drink?" he asked. "You must have something."

"I would like anything you are having," she smiled.

He thought she was behaving very sensibly and was trusting him in a way he found almost pathetic, and then he realised that she had no idea of the trouble she might have been in if she had fallen into other hands.

There were men who would have exploited anyone so pretty and they made money from less pleasant visitors who were looking for loose women.

And there were also men who would have taken her straight round to the front of her father's house and expect to be rewarded for saving her from falling into the water.

'She is so young and innocent," the Prince said to himself. 'She is also defenceless and there is nothing I can do but look after her.'

He took her a glass of red wine that he thought was better than most of the other drinks obtainable.

Then the Prince asked the publican what he could give them for supper.

The two men in the bar thanked him for the drinks he had bought them and wished him goodnight and were obviously delighted at a free drink from a visitor.

"They're surprised at you bein' so generous," the publican said as they left through the open door. "Most tourists as comes here and there ain't many, never spend a lira more than they can help."

"Well, I have had a bit of luck lately. That is why I brought my sister here to enjoy the beauty of Venice. As we are both hungry, I am quite prepared to pay whatever you ask for the best meal you can possibly provide."

The publican's eyes lit up and again he disappeared towards the kitchen.

He came back to announce,

"Me wife says she'll have somethin' for you to eat that'll be real tasty in about twenty minutes. If you'd like to go upstairs, I'll show you to your rooms and you can lie on your beds while you're waitin'."

"That is a good idea because we are both tired and if you will find me the finest white wine you have, we will enjoy it at dinner."

"You be a real gentleman after me own heart and I promise you what my wife be cookin' be worth eatin'."

"I feel sure it will be, but first, do you have decent accommodation for our two horses?"

The publican assured the Prince that he had and that there was a lad who would look after them.

He led them up some rough stairs to where there were two bedrooms, one on each side of the passage. They were small rooms and neither of them properly furnished.

There was just a bed and bare boards on the floors, but to the Prince's surprise both the rooms were clean. The windows had obviously been opened since they arrived and the rooms did not smell as musty as he had feared.

"These rooms will do us splendidly," he said to the publican, "and we are very grateful to you for having us."

"You'll have a good night's rest and be fine in the mornin', sir. I'll give you a shout when supper's ready."

"Thank you very much."

The Prince went into the room opposite his where he found Sacia looking out of the window.

"I am sure no one would think of finding me here," she whispered.

"I am afraid you will not be very comfortable, but at least you are safe. I am quite sure no one will be looking for you so far afield or in a place like this."

Suddenly Sacia laughed.

"It's all so funny," she cried, "and so extraordinary. It's like a story in a book!"

"That is the best way to view it and tomorrow we will make plans of where we will go and what you can do."

She was suddenly still and her eyes grew wide.

"You're not trying to tell me – I should go back?"

It flashed through the Prince's mind just how much he had been pushed into inviting Princess Marziale to stay.

"I promise you one thing," he said, "I will not ask you to do anything you don't want to do. I will only advise you on what I think will keep you safe and happy."

"Thank you, thank you, Nico. You are so kind and wonderful. I think you are an archangel sent down from Heaven to protect me."

"I have never been suspected of being an archangel before, but I am quite willing to try to be one!"

"I don't think you have to try," she replied, "I think it just comes naturally!"

Then they were both laughing and the Prince added,

"I must congratulate you, Sacia. You have behaved so wonderfully well in peculiar and trying circumstances. Let's hope we will both escape tomorrow."

"Are you really running away too?" she quizzed.

"Just as much as you are and that is why I am so sympathetic."

"You have been brilliant, absolutely brilliant," she sighed, "and as you have just said, no one would ever think of looking for me here."

The Prince knew he might say the same of himself, but it would be wrong to talk too much about himself.

"I am going to wash before supper," he now said and went back into his room.

CHAPTER THREE

After a surprisingly well-cooked supper of fried fish and local cheeses the Prince went out to see that the horses were comfortable.

Both he and Sacia had slept well and came down to breakfast early. It was what the publican and his wife had anticipated.

As soon as they sat down at the table, the breakfast, which was simple but good, was put in front of them.

Needless to say the publican's wife was curious and as soon as she had finished in the kitchen, she came and talked to them while they ate.

This meant they could not plan where they would now go and it was only after they had finished eating and the Prince had paid the bill that they were alone.

They said their goodbyes and walked to the stable at the back of the house.

"I have something to say to you," murmured Sacia.

"What is it?" the Prince asked her.

"I thought of where I could go and where I will not only be safe but could earn some money of my own."

The Prince looked at her.

She was so beautiful and so young in the morning sunlight and he just thought that it was wrong for anyone so lovely to have to work for a living.

"I am listening – "

"When I was at my Convent School in Rome," she began, "we had a teacher who came in to instruct those who took extra lessons in Greek."

The Prince stared at her in astonishment.

"Are you telling me you can speak Greek?"

"Yes, and I know Classical Greek too."

"I don't think even scholars speak classical Greek. There would be no one to talk to!"

The Prince could speak modern Greek himself and because of his great interest in the ancient Gods, especially Aphrodite, he had made an effort to learn Classical Greek.

But he had never known a woman who had learnt it too and he found it hard to believe her.

"My teacher said I was the best pupil she had ever had," Sacia was saying, "and I am sure she was very fond of me. She would let me work with her. Perhaps, if she has as many pupils as she had then, I could earn a little."

"What is really important now, Sacia, is that you have somewhere to hide so of course we will certainly go to Rome and see her. What we have to do is go across to the Western coast and find a ship to take us there."

It was all very difficult.

If, as he anticipated, her parents were searching for her, people would soon learn that she had disappeared and they would be only too ready to search for her if they were offered a reward.

'I wonder who she is?' he thought again to himself and then he felt that was irrelevant at the moment.

What he must do is to spirit her away to safety just as he too wanted to feel safe.

They saddled the horses.

"Now we can really start moving," he remarked. "Although it will take us quite a time to reach Rome, it should not be as difficult as one might think."

"You are so good to me, Nico. At the same time I cannot expect you to worry about me. How could I have been so stupid as not to have brought any money with me or for that matter *any clothes*."

The Prince chuckled.

"I guessed that you would be worrying about your clothes sooner or later. It will be very annoying to have to wear the same dress day after day.

"If you and I can find a shop, which I rather doubt out here, I will advance you any money you might require, and then when you are making your fortune by teaching rather stupid children to speak Greek, you can pay me back."

He was joking and Sacia laughed.

"You may have to wait a very long time!"

"I am prepared to do so," he replied.

When he first went downstairs he had been sensible enough to order a picnic luncheon and the publican and his wife had been only too pleased to oblige him.

"If we don't eat it all at luncheon time," the Prince had said to Sacia, "we can always keep it for supper and who knows where we might have to sleep."

As they rode on he talked to her about Greece and he found that she knew a great deal about the Greek Gods and

Goddesses and all about the teaching of Socrates, who with the brilliant philosophers who followed him, Plato and Aristotle, had made Athens into the most brilliant and intellectual City of the ancient world.

Yet what he appreciated more than anything else was that she did not chatter, and unless he wished to talk to her, she was silent.

She looked so glorious in the sunshine that he could understand why her parents were so determined she should make a grand marriage, whatever her private feelings about it might be.

The Prince had chosen unfrequented roads across the country that was sparsely inhabited.

After they had ridden some way, he commented,

"I don't know exactly where we are now, but we are certainly going in the right direction."

Sacia gave a cry of delight.

"I'm sure that's right. I am now not only further away from those searching for me, but they would never think for one moment that this is where I could manage to go on my own."

The Prince thought, seeing how lovely she was, that there would always have been someone to help her, but he did not say it aloud for fear of agitating her.

There was little sign of life where they were and when they stopped because they were feeling hungry, there was not a house in sight.

"I wonder who this land belongs to?" Sacia asked.

"I expect it is something we will never know. It might be a mistake to ask too many questions."

*

They set off again after their picnic luncheon.

At four o'clock in the afternoon the Prince stopped.

"I think that there's a house over there amongst the trees," he said, "but I cannot see it very clearly. It might be where we can stay the night. Shall we go and explore?"

"Let's," agreed Sacia. "Perhaps it is a farmhouse, although there does not seem to have been much work put into these fields."

"I am rather surprised, as you live in a town, that you know so much about the country."

"Oh, Papa owns a country house as well as one in Venice and we move between one and the other because he regularly gets bored. Not only with where we are living but with the people we see day after day."

The Prince longed to ask her questions as to who her father was, but he sensed that it was not the right time. Moreover he had no wish to tell her anything about himself in return.

They rode on slowly crossing some fields and then dismounted to lead their horses through the wood that hid the house they were approaching.

Then very suddenly two men who looked as though they might be gamekeepers came striding towards them.

"Where're you goin' and what're you doin' 'ere?" one of the men asked in very rough Italian.

63

"We are travellers," the Prince responded, "and we hope to find an inn where my sister and I can obtain food and lodging."

"You be trespassing," the other man added, "and you must come with us and we'll take you to the owner who don't allow likes of you to be walkin' over his land."

"I will explain to him," replied the Prince, "that if we have done anything wrong it is only through ignorance and we are strangers to this part of Italy."

"That's what they all says when they're sneakin' our birds or our stags."

The Prince thought it wise not to answer this.

As the two men started walking on either side of them, Sacia's hand crept into his.

"It's all right," he said speaking in Greek, which he knew only she would understand. "We will apologise to the owner of this land and I hope there is a village not far away from here where we can stay the night."

They had not gone far before he looked ahead with astonishment.

There was a large and impressive Castle just ahead of them.

It was surrounded not only by a moat but also by a vast garden with flowerbeds full of flowers in bloom and there was a flag flying from the turret of the Castle.

The Prince was aware that whoever the owner was he was a man of some consequence.

He next tried frantically to remember if any of his father's friends lived in this district and then he wondered if on his numerous travels he had met anyone who came from this part of the world.

However he could not think of anyone and he felt it best not to ask any questions of the two men who were clearly guarding the property and would have instructions as to what to do with people who trespassed on it.

They crossed the moat and into a large courtyard beyond it, stopping outside what was obviously a side door and not the main entrance.

"Now stay 'ere," one of the men hissed, "while I go and tell the Duca what I've found you doin'."

"Tell him we have no wish to do anything wrong," the Prince stipulated, "we were in fact merely resting after making a long journey."

He was not certain if the man understood what he had said or wished to. He did not answer but disappeared through the heavy oak door.

There were steps up to it and Sacia sat down.

"Whatever happens," she whispered to the Prince, "the Duca must *not* know who I am."

"As *I* don't know, I see no reason why *he* should!"

"We must not use my real name, always call me Noemi," she said nervously. "If Papa is making everyone in Venice look for me, Sacia is a name they will remember. And if the Duca who lives here is very grand, he may know Papa."

Looking at him with anxiety in her large eyes, he thought no one could look lovelier. She had a fairy-like appearance which was accentuated by the heavy stonework of the Castle.

"And I must be in disguise as well," the Prince added, "so I will call myself 'Tias', which you will admit is easy to remember."

"We have decided on Nanny's name for me and I feel sure as she is in the next world that she will not allow us to get into too much mischief!"

The Prince chuckled as he surmised that no one he had met would be as calm and sensible in the same arduous circumstances as Sacia.

He was actually rather worried himself.

The Duca, whoever he was, might have seen him at some ceremony and remember what he looked like.

He had in fact attended a number of conferences and meetings since becoming Ruler of Vienz, and usually he had to listen to long and exceptionally boring speeches by Princes from small and insignificant Principalities.

They were determined to make their own point of view heard and they were the ones most likely to suffer if they were not friendly with the greater powers. Therefore the Prince had known it was his duty to be present.

Now he tried very hard to tell himself that he was being unnecessarily concerned.

Nevertheless, when the man who had gone into the Castle reappeared, he drew in his breath.

"The Duca wishes to see you," he blurted out, "now you follow me!"

At the same time a groom came to hold the horses and Sacia rose from the step.

She and the Prince walked behind one of the men who led the way, while the other followed behind almost as if he was afraid they might make a run for it.

The Castle inside was luxuriously furnished and the Prince noted that it must belong to someone not only of distinction but also plenty of money.

There was no doubt that much money had been spent not just on the furniture but on the Castle's upkeep.

They passed a number of servants all dressed in a smart livery and they had obviously been trained not to stare.

The Prince guessed they were now in the centre of the Castle and it was even larger than he had first thought.

Then there were two huge doors ahead and the man ahead of them held up his hand for them to stop.

Then he went in through the door closing it behind him.

He came out almost immediately and called out,

"Come in."

He spoke abruptly with an exaggerated arrogance and it told the Prince he was afraid of his employer.

Holding Sacia by the hand they walked into a large and exquisitely furnished drawing room.

The walls were decorated with fine pictures and on one side there were a number of bookshelves.

Seated at a large desk with gold candlesticks and an elaborate gold inkpot was a middle-aged man, whose hair was just going grey.

One look at him told the Prince he was well aware of his own importance and that he was prepared to frighten anyone who came in front of him either as a poacher or a thief.

The Prince took his hand from Sacia's and walked forward towards the Duca.

"I must apologise most sincerely," he began, "for apparently trespassing on your land. But my sister and I were riding across the country and actually did not know exactly where we were. I am so sorry that your men had to bring us here, but we had no idea until we saw your Castle that such a magnificent monument was hidden from us by the trees."

The Duca was listening to the Prince.

At the same time his eyes were on Sacia.

"You tell me you are brother and sister," he said, "but you have omitted to give me your name."

With a quickness of mind that was characteristic of him, the Prince replied,

"I am Count Tias Fleury, and my sister's name is Noemi."

"Then I have met members of your family," the Duca responded.

The Prince smiled.

"There are a very large number of them."

He had chosen the name Fleury knowing it was an aristocratic name and that there were a great many of them scattered all over Italy.

The Duca rose.

"Instead of accusing you of trespassing," he said, "may I welcome you to my Castle and if you are travelling I hope you will honour me by staying the night."

"That is extremely kind of you and it is something we should enjoy. I am overwhelmed by your majestic Castle and especially by your pictures."

"They are not as beautiful," the Duca replied, "as your sister."

He held out his hand to Sacia as he spoke.

She dropped him a deep curtsy before she took it.

The Prince thought it was very graceful of her.

"As you have been travelling, I gather for some time," the Duca continued, "I suggest perhaps you would like to wash your hands and then we will have tea on the terrace from which on a clear day you can see the sea."

He was speaking to Sacia, who answered,

"I would love to do that. Thank you very much for not sending us away from your fantastic Castle. I should have been very sad if I had had to miss it."

It was obvious that the Duca was delighted at her remarks.

When he rang the bell, he started to tell Sacia about his collection of pictures. They were, he boasted, one of the best private collections in the whole of Italy.

"I say it with confidence, though there are doubtless people who will contradict me," he said. "After you have had tea you will see for yourself if I am right or wrong."

"I would love to, but in the meantime I would like to make myself tidy or I feel that your ancestors will look down disapprovingly on me!"

The Duca laughed at this and then the Prince asked if their horses could be looked after and his saddlebags brought in.

The Duca immediately gave instructions for this to be done and they were taken by a formidable housekeeper up the stairs.

Sacia was shown into the first State bedroom with its huge canopied bed and it was very different from where she had slept the previous night.

The Prince's room was next door.

They were told when they had tidied themselves a servant would be waiting to take them to the terrace where they would be served tea.

The Prince washed his hands and brushed his hair with the brush that Texxo had put in the bag for him.

Then he took his brush and comb and went into the room next door and, as he expected, Sacia was sitting at the dressing table trying to put her auburn hair into place.

"I should have thought of it last night, Sacia, and you should have asked me, but I have a comb here and a brush that I believe you will need."

"Of course I do and thank you. I did think of it this morning, but you were in such a hurry to leave that, if I had spent too much time titivating myself, then you would have been annoyed."

"You are so unlike most women, and may I tell you that despite two days of travelling your dress does not look creased or at all dirty."

"I had to sponge quite a lot of the marks off it last night," admitted Sacia.

Then she glanced at the door to make quite sure it was closed before she murmured,

"You were so clever in making us sound important, otherwise I am quite certain he would have sent us away."

She gave a little giggle before she added,

"And I am sure he was impressed by your supposed title."

"I had to think quickly, Sacia, as I was not looking forward to spending the night in a dungeon!"

Sacia gave a little cry.

"Do you think he would have put me in one too?"

"Nothing would surprise me. "Remember, as a Duca he considers himself very significant and thus the more you curtsy and flatter him the more comfortable we will be."

Sacia laughed.

"I think that applies to most men – even you?"

He liked the way she was teasing him and told her,

"We are certainly having an adventure and finding you, Sacia, is the biggest excitement I have had for a long time."

"We can only hope it does not end in tears, which inevitably my escapades did when I was a child."

The Prince put out his hand.

"Come along. You look lovely and the Duca will undoubtedly tell you so."

"I cannot help wishing, Nico, that we were having tea alone. And if we are staying the night, we would be able to talk at dinner as we did last night."

"But the beds will be very comfortable and the food delicious and the wines will be completely different from last night's fare."

"I am sure, Nanny, if she was with us, would say you think too much about your tummy!" Sacia teased him. "Now let's go downstairs and see the Duca's pictures."

The Prince was astonished that she could talk so lightly and so amusingly.

He was quite certain any other woman would still have been suffering from the shock of being more or less arrested.

However, he said nothing and they were escorted downstairs by a powdered footman.

The Castle was indeed even more impressive than the Duca had told them it would be and his pictures, the Prince had to admit, were superb.

But what interested him most was that Sacia knew so much about them and the artists.

He supposed that when she was at school in Rome the girls had spent a great deal of time in the art galleries and she had certainly benefitted by the opportunity.

She guessed the name of several artists before the Duca could tell her and she was invariably right. She had an appreciation of his pictures that delighted their owner.

Tea on the terrace was an elaborate affair.

The Duca explained that many of his guests at the Castle were English and several of his family had actually married English women.

So he was in the habit of having what the Italians call 'English Tea' at half-past four.

There was certainly a great deal to eat and, as their improvised luncheon had only been sandwiches and fruit, both the Prince and Sacia enjoyed themselves.

After tea was finished Sacia went upstairs to her bedroom to lie down and the Duca took the Prince to view his Armoury and to see how the drawbridge worked as it had done for centuries.

"I hope you are not anticipating that you will have to raise it against an enemy," the Prince remarked jokingly.

"One never knows," the Duca replied. "And I will fight to the finish if anyone attempts to take my land or my Castle away from me."

"I am sure no one will try to do so."

At the same time there had been rumours of more revolutions in Italy and the Prince well knew that his own people were always apprehensive of what might happen in the future.

If there was a takeover of smaller Principalities, the predator might easily turn his attention to Vienz.

Sacia could not change her dress for dinner, but a bath was brought into her room and while she was having it, the housekeeper arranged to have her dress sponged and pressed.

"That's a very pretty gown," the housekeeper said, "and if you take my advice, ma'am, you'll buy yourself something simple and washable."

Sacia hesitated for a moment and then asked,

"I don't suppose you have one hidden away in the Castle. My brother would gladly buy it for me."

"As it happens, ma'am, I've just finished making one for my granddaughter and I thinks that she's about the same size as you."

"Oh, please sell it to me," Sacia begged. "I should be so grateful."

"I'll put it here in your room so that you can see it when you comes up to bed, ma'am," she promised.

Sacia then knocked on the Prince's door.

When he called out, "come in," she entered.

"Please, Nico, will you lend me some money to buy a gown? I am not quite certain what I will have to pay for it, but the housekeeper has one that she had made for her granddaughter and she will let me buy it."

"You look as if you have been offered the Koh-I-Noor," the Prince smiled.

"I want to look pretty for you when you have been so good to me."

He gave Sacia some notes and she hurried back to her room and the housekeeper was delighted.

"That's more than enough, ma'am, and I'll easily make my granddaughter another one for her birthday."

"You are so kind and I am very grateful."

The housekeeper then helped Sacia to arrange her hair.

When she went down to dinner still wearing her old dress, she looked, the Prince thought, like a flower just coming into bloom.

Because she was no longer nervous she talked away endlessly to the Duca during the meal.

She made him laugh and was, at the same time, the Prince considered, extremely intelligent.

Only when they had moved into the drawing room and drank their coffee did the Duca remark,

"I know you have a long journey in front of you, but you should reach the coast in three days at the most."

"Do you think," the Prince asked, "we will be able to find a ship to take us down to Rome?"

"I am sure you will. There should be no difficulty in reaching Rome or anywhere else you wish to go."

"That sounds excellent," the Prince enthused.

There was more information he wanted to obtain from the Duca, but he was obviously very charmed with Sacia and insisted on talking to her.

She was astute at drawing him out on his favourite interests whilst praising the Castle and its contents.

The Prince reflected that she must have had a good deal of practice with her father and his friends.

He could not remember a girl of her age having so much to say or being so intelligent not only in what she related but in handling the man listening to her.

When girls of her age had come to the Palace, he had invariably found them incredibly dull and he had made every excuse not to have them sitting next to him at a meal.

But now the Duca was listening intently to Sacia as if he found every word she uttered entrancing.

The Prince felt that they were certainly paying for the hospitality they were gratefully receiving.

"I am afraid we must go to bed early," he said as soon as politeness allowed, "as we have a long way to go tomorrow, we should start as soon as possible."

"I will order breakfast for you at seven o'clock and you must forgive me if I don't appear until later," the Duca replied.

"We will want to say goodbye to you," said Sacia, "and to thank you for all your kindness."

"But it is you who have been kind to me," the Duca insisted. "I am often very lonely here even though I have my pictures to keep me company."

"I am sure if you listen to them they will talk to you just as well if not better than we can," Sacia told him.

"I will remember you said that to me, Noemi."

As they said goodnight, he kissed Sacia's hand and she curtsied to him again.

Then she and the Prince walked on up the stairs to their bedrooms.

The Prince went into Sacia's room with her to see that everything was in order for her.

She was ecstatic at the very pretty new dress that was waiting for her on a chair.

"You will be surprised how different I will look tomorrow, Nico. This dress is much too heavy to be worn riding and I was only made to put it on to impress the man who was coming to propose to me."

She gave a little shiver as she spoke and the Prince admonished her sharply,

"Forget him! Don't think about it! Every mile we travel we will be further away from him."

"I know, Nico, and you are being so very kind and wonderful to me. And what is more, I am enjoying every moment of it!"

She smiled at him.

He wondered if he should kiss her goodnight on the cheek as a brother would have done.

Then he told himself it would be a mistake as he might scare her as so far she had not been the slightest bit frightened of him.

He walked to the door as he remembered that the Duca had kissed her hand and it was something he should not have done to an unmarried girl.

He turned back.

"Don't forget to lock your door," he urged her.

Sacia's eyes widened.

"Lock my door, but why? We are not in a hotel and it is something I have never done in a private house."

"You are in a strange Castle now, Sacia, and I want you to lock it."

He looked at the lock on the door as he spoke and then he realised that the key was not there.

He looked down to see if it had fallen on the floor, but there was no sign of it.

Without saying anything he walked next door to his own room.

Opening the door he looked at the lock and as he expected the key was there.

He went back to Sacia.

"We are changing rooms," he announced, "collect your things and move into mine."

She looked at him in astonishment.

"Why?" she asked, "I like this room and I am sure the bed is very comfortable."

"Perhaps it is, but it's always right to lock yourself in. I should have told you last night."

"Mama always made me lock my room when we were staying in a hotel, but, as I said, I have never done so in a private house. I expect if the key is not in the lock, it has been lost."

"Well, fortunately we don't have much to move," the Prince persisted. "I will fetch my bag."

As he spoke he went to fetch it and he pushed into it his sponge and a few other items he had used while he was having a bath before dinner.

When he went back to Sacia, she had collected her new dress as well as his comb and brush.

"I still think you are being a little foolish," she said, as she went into his room. "I just cannot imagine anyone would come into my room in the Castle."

"You never know," the Prince warned. "There are a large number of men below. I saw them when the Duca took me to the Armoury."

"I had forgotten them, Nico, but I am sure that they would be far too frightened of the Duca to insult one of his guests."

"I will not allow you to take any risks, Sacia, now goodnight, lock the door and when I wake at six-thirty, I will knock and you can let me in."

"Goodnight, Nico, and I am praying that we will be as lucky tomorrow as we have been today."

The Prince smiled.

"I am sure your prayers will be heard and I will add mine to them."

"It is so very very exciting being with you," Sacia enthused.

The Prince left the room and stood outside until he heard her turn the key.

Then he went into the room that had been assigned to Sacia, undressed and climbed into bed.

He took one item from his bag he had not bothered with the night before and put it under his pillow.

It was his revolver.

Then he blew out the candles and the room was in darkness.

An hour later he was sure that Sacia was sleeping and it would be expected that he was too.

He heard the door opening very quietly.

The Prince closed his eyes.

He became aware that someone was walking slowly across the carpet to the bed.

There was a candle in the hand of the newcomer and only as he reached the bed did he realise who was in it.

For a moment he stood very still as if he found it hard to believe his eyes.

Then slowly and silently he went back the way he had come.

The Prince did not move.

The door closed quietly behind the intruder.

He was aware that the footsteps he could still hear had stopped outside the door next to his.

If hands tried to open the door, he could not hear it and he remembered with satisfaction he had heard the key turn in the lock.

Then there was complete silence.

He turned over, closed his eyes and went to sleep.

CHAPTER FOUR

The next morning the Prince and Sacia departed before the Duca had come down to breakfast.

They went to the stables and asked for their horses to be saddled.

Then, having tipped the grooms, they led them over the drawbridge and through the wood.

When they reached the open fields by which they had approached the Castle last night, the Prince helped Sacia to mount her horse and he mounted his.

"That was very unexpected," Sacia piped up, "and we never guessed when we thought we were looking for a small house that we would find that huge Castle."

"It was certainly interesting," the Prince agreed, "and I very much admired the Duca's pictures."

"So did I and as you were so fascinated by them it is obvious to me that you have some of your own."

"I have a few," the Prince admitted.

He guessed she was longing to ask him questions, but thought he might think her curious and did not wish to seem inquisitive.

They must remain anonymous to each other until he found her a safe hiding place.

He was thinking it was lucky his instinct as well as his eyes had warned him what the Duca might attempt last night.

He had noticed how much he was admiring Sacia and then he had the idea that he was not often alone in his Castle whatever he might say about how much he enjoyed his pictures and his books.

'I suppose,' the Prince said somewhat frantically to himself, 'it was one *roué* recognising another!'

At any rate he had rescued Sacia and he was glad that they were escaping without any undue unpleasantness – it might easily have been a very different story.

They rode as far as possible on rough roads in the direction of the high mountains and deliberately avoided all towns.

They stopped for a quick luncheon on the way at an inn in a small village.

The food served to them was very poor – the veal was tough with no vegetables and the bread was stale.

"This is a bit different from last night!" said Sacia.

She was not grumbling at all, but laughing and the Prince appreciated how good she had been so far on the journey in never complaining.

He had travelled in far greater comfort with other women who found fault at the slightest inconvenience and then they would draw attention to themselves by forcing him to pay them endless compliments.

He wondered if it was the way Sacia had been trained since she was a child or whether it came naturally and by the end of the day he was certain that naturally was the right answer.

She was, he was sure, very sensitive to what other people said or felt and he would not have been surprised if he found that she was clairvoyant.

They had ridden some way from the inn when the Prince asked her,

"What do you think is happening at your home?"

Sacia flinched.

"I think everyone my father employs and probably others are all searching for me. They will have dragged the Canal just in case my body was still there. But they will never guess that I was lucky enough to find you!"

"It was certainly a very unconventional meeting."

"I think my Guardian Angel had sent you there although you were not aware of it."

"I was asking *my* Guardian Angel to give me an adventure and he has certainly answered *my* prayer!"

"He?" Sacia questioned. "How can you be so sure it's not a beautiful lady angel watching over you?"

"Then I think that must be you, Sacia, and if I am in trouble I will expect you to rescue *me*."

Sacia laughed.

"I should have thought you were too clever to fall into a trap or even, as we feared yesterday, to be arrested for trespassing."

"I think we were very lucky to escape as easily as we did."

He was thinking that if the Duca had found Sacia in the room from which he had removed the key, they might have had a very different story to tell.

83

He could in fact understand that the Duca had not for a moment believed that Sacia was his sister and he had thought when he introduced her that there was a look of suspicion in his eyes.

It was obvious to the Prince that from the moment the Duca had decided to take Sacia from him, he would have been prepared to bribe her to agree.

She was outstandingly pretty – glorious was really the right word.

She was also intelligent and the Duca had quite obviously thought, if she was really the sister of a Count, she would not have been travelling about alone with him, as there would have been a lady's maid and doubtless an older woman to take care of her.

'Well, we did avoid that pitfall rather easily,' the Prince pondered. 'But I must be very much more careful of Sacia than I thought necessary until now.'

He gazed at her sitting gracefully on her horse.

She was clearly extremely happy, looking eagerly ahead and from side to side as they rode on and he thought that any great artist would have been thrilled to paint her portrait.

He himself would always remember how beautiful she was and he wondered when he left her with her teacher in Rome where he would then go.

Sooner or later he would have to consider returning home.

He would have to give Ruta time, if he was clever, to make the most of his new title.

Then he would be forthright enough to make it very clear that the Prince Nicolo of Vienz had not the slightest intention of getting married.

And so the Princess's father might accept Ruta.

Ruta was in any case a rich man. His family had an estate in the North of the country where, the Prince knew, they were of great social influence.

The Comte had actually suggested to him that he should come and stay there for the next shooting season and he had provisionally agreed that it would be enjoyable.

If he went there, the Prince knew that the whole neighbourhood would go out of their way to entertain and amuse him.

He was indeed certain that Ruta and the Princess were very much in love with each other and she would be exceedingly happy with Ruta if her father allowed her to marry him.

'If I have done nothing else,' the Prince thought as he remembered the conversation he had overheard, 'I have at least made two people happy and that should be a good mark in my favour.'

"You are very looking serious," Sacia quizzed him. "What are you thinking about, Nico?"

The Prince had for the moment forgotten her and then without thinking, he answered her,

"I was thinking of marriage."

"I thought that was why you had run away."

"Did I tell you that?" the Prince asked.

"No, you just said you had run away, but I guessed because you are so good-looking that there must be many women who continually pursue you."

"Now how could you think that about me?"

She looked rather shy before replying,

"Maybe I am being inquisitive and should not have said that. But it is obvious that you are an aristocrat and, from what I have seen of my father's friends and of Papa himself, they are always thinking about marriage and who they would unite with whom."

"Which is what they have done in your case – "

Sacia shuddered.

"It was not originally Papa's idea. He was trying to find me someone young but naturally from a distinguished family."

"So it is the other man's fault you are now in this predicament," the Prince remarked.

Sacia shuddered again.

"I don't think Papa had thought of anyone who was so old and at the time so important. But of course he and all my other relations thought how fortunate I was to have the chance of marrying someone so distinguished."

The Prince was racking his brains as to who this person might be.

Actually he had never been particularly interested on his visits to Venice in calling on the numerous families who he had always understood gave themselves airs and graces.

Now he was curious as to who was pursuing Sacia and before he could speak, she suggested,

"We are so happy as we are without knowing much about each other. Please let it stay that way."

"Of course, if that is what you want, Sacia."

"If we begin to reveal why we are here and tell each other exactly why we have run away, then I am sure all the misery and fear will come back again."

She smiled before she continued,

"I have been so ecstatic since you saved my life and so very kindly took me away with you."

"Let's talk about other things, Sacia, and I promise I will try not to be curious about you as long as you are not curious about me."

Sacia gave a laugh.

"Of course I am intrigued about you, but I cannot believe, as you are a man, that your predicament is as bad as mine."

She threw up her hands.

"Anyway don't let's talk about it. When I think about what I have left behind, I feel as if a deep black cloud is creeping over me. At any moment I may wake up and find this is all a dream."

"I assure you it is very real and may I say that I think you are behaving wonderfully well in very difficult circumstances. In a crisis most women scream and burst into tears!"

"I know that only too well, Nico, and I have learnt not to cry except when I am alone."

The Prince thought if she did cry she would look so pathetic and at the same time so beautiful that it would be impossible for any man not to sweep her into his arms and kiss her.

That evening they found a small inn in a village in the foothills of the Apennines where they had quite a well-cooked supper and a reasonably comfortable night.

*

The next day they took a packed lunch with them and spent the day crossing the Northern slopes of the high mountains by a route that was easier than they might have expected.

On the way they spent the next night in another inn in a mountain village, which was much less comfortable.

They were told that they would reach the sea the next afternoon.

Feeling exhausted they rode down to find quite a large harbour and a number of fishermen standing about.

The Prince pulled in his horse and enquired,

"Will you please tell me exactly where I am?"

One man told him the name of the small fishing village and then the Prince spoke to another who seemed a little less rough than the others,

"I am wondering," he said, "if there is any chance of finding a ship here to take us to Rome."

The fishermen looked at each other as if they were not sure of the answer and then one of them chipped in,

"I've got a friend who expects a ship to be stoppin' here tomorrow as he be goin' South."

"That is good news and I hope there will be a place for me and my sister on board."

"I be sure there'll be a place for anyone as pretty as her."

The Prince ignored this comment and continued,

"As my sister and I will be staying the night, maybe you will advise me of the most comfortable inn here?"

There was some altercation about his request and finally they told him the name of an inn that was a short distance away from the village itself.

The Prince thanked them and picked up his reins and as they rode off they heard the fishermen talking about them and making complimentary remarks about Sacia.

"The trouble with you," the Prince murmured, "is that you are far too pretty!"

Sacia laughed.

"I am glad someone thinks so. I did not receive many compliments at home. But then my mother was an acknowledged beauty and my elder sister has been painted by several famous artists."

"Has anyone painted you, Sacia?"

"Not yet, but I always hoped one of the artists who come to Venice would want to paint my portrait. But they are always too busy painting San Marco or the Rialto."

The Prince chuckled.

"It's a very sad story and they will continue to paint them long after you have joined the angels in Heaven."

"If I ever do join them, but by the time I die I may be sent to hell to do penance for my sins."

"Have you committed many?"

"It will be considered a great sin by my family that I have run away and disappeared. I expect I will have to be penitent for that for the rest of my life."

"I doubt it, Sacia. You will marry someone you really love and nothing will matter except that you and he will be happy ever after."

Sacia clasped her hands together.

"Oh, I do so hope that comes true! It's what I pray for every night, as I told you, not only to God, but also to Aphrodite."

"Then I hope she listens to us both."

"I want you to tell me – " Sacia began.

The Prince knew she wanted to talk about Greek Goddesses, but at that moment they reached what he was sure was the inn they had been informed about.

It was not very prepossessing, but it obviously was large enough to take in a few tourists and the Prince only hoped that there would be empty rooms for them.

When they went inside, the publican was somewhat impressed by their appearances and he said that he had two rooms available but only for one night and he could stable their horses.

The rooms had been booked for people who were arriving the next day by ship.

"Is this ship for tourists?" the Prince asked him.

"I don't know, sir. It were two people who were here last week and went to Lucca and asked if they could come back tomorrow."

The Prince considered that this told him nothing, but he had to accept the rooms.

He decided that he must find out more accurately if any ships were likely to come into the fishing village, and he knew the ships that came from France carrying tourists usually sailed directly to Rome or Naples.

If there was not one due soon, they would have to find another way of reaching Rome.

However for tonight at least there would be a roof over their heads.

They were shown the rooms, which were small and exceedingly badly furnished, but as before not dirty.

The Prince had travelled enough to know that some inns calling themselves hotels could be most unpleasant.

"I am afraid we are not going to be particularly comfortable," he said to Sacia as they looked at the rooms. "But we cannot expect the comfort we enjoyed with the Duca to be available every day like manna from Heaven!"

"I am quite happy as long as I am with you, Nico, and one thing I can be quite sure of is that no one Papa sends in search of me is likely to look in a place like this."

"I might say the same for myself!"

"Then we should be grateful that we are both safe and don't have to worry about someone pouncing on us out of the dark."

The Prince thought that could easily have happened to her at the Duca's Castle and yet he had no intention of telling her, so he merely replied,

"We will hope to find something decent to eat and then we will go to bed."

Sacia nodded as he continued,

"I will try and find out about the ship that may be stopping here tomorrow, but these people appear to know very little about it."

Only after he had sent Sacia up to bed did he ask the publican to make enquiries about the ship and he had thought of going down to the harbour himself.

But he did not like to leave Sacia alone even though there were very few people in the inn, only occasional men coming in for a cheap drink.

What the Prince did eventually find out was that the ship would put into the harbour at about noon.

It was coming from Genoa and he was assured that the ship's destination was Rome and that was where he had to escort Sacia.

When he went up to bed, the Prince found the straw mattress was extremely hard and although he opened the window wide the room still smelt musty.

It was in every way the sort of place that he most disliked and yet once again before he fell asleep he could not help thinking how fascinating it all was.

Sacia had not complained to him nor said anything derogatory about any of their lodgings.

He recalled various times in the past when a pretty woman had been angry with him for not providing her with some small but unnecessary comfort and had made it clear he had not been caring for her as he should have been.

'Sacia is surely a very good travelling companion,' the Prince mused as he turned over.

The bed felt just as hard as it had on his other side and the pillow too was very lumpy and then he told himself that as a soldier and Ruler he should not be upset by trivial unimportant discomforts.

He should just fix his mind on achieving what he had set out to do and then he recalled that he could not be sure of what that was until he returned home.

He wondered if they were in a panic because they could not find him and hoped that Ruta was making the most of his disappearance.

Then as he fell asleep he was thinking again how beautiful Sacia was and how glad he was that he had been quick-witted enough to save her from the Duca.

*

The following morning there was no hurry as the ship was not due until noon.

They enjoyed a late breakfast that was rather better than their supper had been – the fish had come in fresh and the bread had been baked that morning by the publican's wife.

The Prince paid the reasonable amount they were asked for their rooms and for stabling their horses.

He realised that he would have to dispose of the horses and that the publican was the only local who might buy them, probably with the intention of selling them later at a good profit.

After some hard bargaining, he agreed a price with the publican far below their true worth and he bid a solemn farewell to his favourite stallion.

Then they walked down to the harbour, the Prince carrying his saddlebag.

There were several fishermen around, two of whom they had seen the previous day.

They talked to the Prince and assured him that there was no question of this ship passing by the village as the larger vessels did.

The Prince however was still rather anxious and then Sacia exclaimed,

"There's a ship on the horizon and it looks as if it's coming towards us!"

He gave a sigh of relief.

When the ship came into the harbour, four people appeared who wished to board it and the Prince and Sacia managed to push ahead of them.

There was an Officer who was quite obviously the Purser, although that was a rather grand name for him, who was in charge of the cabins.

Seeing there was a large number of people aboard the ship already, the Prince took the first cabins offered and thankfully there were two of them and they were side by side.

He realised how lucky he had been when the people behind him were told there were only two other cabins left and that they would have to share them.

They were grumbling as Sacia and the Prince went below.

The cabins were small and as bare as a cabin could possibly be. There were no curtains at the window and just blankets on the beds with no sheets.

The Prince then inspected both cabins and neither of them looked better than the other and so he told Sacia that they would just have to put up with what he expected would be considerable discomfort before reaching Rome.

"How long are we at sea?" Sacia enquired.

"I should think it will take us two days," he replied.

"But it is all part of our adventure and we are lucky to be given these two cabins. We will just have to pretend they are more luxurious than they really are."

The Prince laughed.

"You are the sort of travelling companion everyone hopes to find, but is usually disappointed."

"Am I, why?" Sacia asked.

"Because you never complain and accept things as they are," the Prince answered.

"I think the truth is that I am so grateful to you for taking me away with you that I would suffer inexpressible hardship rather than have to go back."

"Then that is all that matters. We can only hope that, if nothing else, they will provide decent meals on this boat."

The Prince's wish was not granted.

The food they were given for dinner was, the Prince considered, completely inedible.

The only consolation was that he was able to buy quite a reasonable bottle of wine – it was apparently far too expensive for the other passengers.

It was the following morning when they stopped at another port that matters became really uncomfortable.

A large number of noisy youths came on board and they had apparently been to some games and having been victors they were celebrating their success.

They started drinking as soon as the ship moved out of harbour and the bar was open. In a few hours they were, the Prince discovered, almost paralytic with the amount of alcohol they had consumed.

Sacia had wanted to stay on deck to watch the land they were passing on their left, but after they had been on deck for a short time the Prince insisted they went below.

It was not so much because the men were drunk, as that he disliked the way they eyed Sacia.

She had always been well protected from ordinary people and very certainly from the sort of men they were mingling with now.

She therefore had no idea that the way they were looking at her was an insult.

"I am sorry," the Prince said when they entered her cabin, "but you are not to come out of here until we reach Rome."

"Why not? Why are you making such a fuss about those men on deck? They are rather noisy and I think they must have drunk a lot, but they are not fighting or making themselves unpleasant."

The Prince reckoned it was only a question of time before they made themselves particularly unpleasant.

"You are to stay here," he repeated. "I think by tonight these youths will be incredibly noisy and you will have no wish to be anywhere near them."

"No, of course not," Sacia agreed.

"Then, Sacia, you must do as I tell you and that incidentally is an *order*!"

She laughed.

"It is nothing new for me to be ordered about, but it is something you have not done until now, Nico."

"I will only do so as long as we are travelling on this ship. You are to stay in this cabin with it locked and barred."

"So I am a prisoner! But I don't really mind, as long as I am *your* prisoner, Nico."

She smiled up at him as she spoke.

The Prince thought she had no idea of how lovely she looked and how much he wanted to kiss her.

Then he told himself it would be a terrible mistake to frighten her or to make her regard him in any different way.

He was sure she meant it when she said she thought he was an archangel who had been sent down from Heaven to rescue her.

She had not seriously thought of him as a man.

He felt certain that she had not seriously considered any man in the past, except of course for the man she was being forced to marry.

'She is completely innocent and unspoilt,' he told himself, 'and that is how she must remain until I leave her.'

He walked to the porthole and looked out.

"It is a fine night and the sea is calm," he said, "so at least those noisy buffoons on deck will not be seasick."

"I want to be outside watching the sun sink in the West and of course I want to see Corsica. I have only seen it on a map with the King of Sardinia beneath it."

"I don't think that they are particularly exciting islands. Not like the islands of Greece."

"Of course not, Nico. Now you are talking about the islands I really want to visit. It would be so exciting if we could go to Delos and Kos – and then on to Delphi."

The Prince smiled.

"I understand exactly why you should want to visit Delphi. Like all women you are dreaming of Apollo and hoping you will meet him in real life."

"How did you guess that? Of course you are right. I have always thought that Apollo was the most thrilling and romantic of all the Greek Gods."

"He was young and handsome, and that, I suppose, is the man every woman hopes to give her heart to," the Prince countered almost sarcastically.

Sacia was silent for a moment and then she parried,

"Apollo conquered the world by the power of his beauty. He had no earthly resources. No Army or Navy and no powerful Government. There was just himself and ever since no one has asked for more."

The Prince believed this to be true.

It was exactly what he was seeking himself and he did not wish to be loved because he was the Ruler of a Kingdom – he wished to be loved as a man.

That was what he had set out to find when he ran away. Then because he was suddenly afraid of his own thoughts, he turned from the window.

"I am going up to see what they are doing," he said. "In the meantime you are to stay here and talk to no one."

"There will be no one to talk to if you leave me," Sacia answered.

He pretended not to hear her and walked from the cabin closing the door quietly.

As he climbed up the companionway he could hear the youths shouting at each other. They were laughing in a way that told him that they were now extremely drunk.

The Prince stayed on deck for a short time and the men, who by now had made it impossible to speak or hear anything but their shouting and laughter, left him alone.

He realised there were very few women on board and those who were, were not young, and no one took any notice of them.

He was however quite certain that if Sacia appeared they would be delighted with her and would undoubtedly frighten her by clustering round her and trying to attract her attention.

He went to see the Purser to ask him if it would be possible for them to have dinner in their own cabins.

"I can understand why you are asking for it, sir," he answered the Prince.

"Do you always have this sort of riotous collection on the ship?" the Prince asked.

"Only once a month when we pick them up at the port we've just left," the Purser replied. "At other times we're fortunate if the ship's half full."

"And you make the journey every week?"

"Every two weeks, sir, and it only pays when we're full like we are today."

"I am just wondering," the Prince asked him, "if it would be wise for my sister, who is young and very pretty, to come out of her cabin before we actually go ashore."

"If you take my advice, sir, you leave her where she is. This lot don't mean any harm, but they drink too much and on one voyage, because of their goings-on, a woman fell into the sea and we had a job to save her."

"I am glad to hear she did not drown."

"She wasn't far off it," the Purser answered, "and I doubt if she'll go to sea again in a hurry."

"Well, that is certainly something we must avoid. So, although you are busy, will you please instruct your Stewards to bring dinner for my sister and myself to her cabin? I am prepared to pay extra for their trouble."

At the mention of extra money the Purser was only too pleased to arrange for their dinner to be carried to Sacia's cabin.

When the Prince put quite a number of coins in his hand, he was overcome and promised he would arrange everything for seven-thirty.

The Prince, pleased at what he had achieved, went back to Sacia.

She was sitting at the porthole and jumped up when he opened the door.

"I have been hoping you would not be long, Nico. The noise is deafening and I am sure those young men are very rough. They might knock you overboard by mistake."

"I quite agree with you, Sacia, and that is why I have arranged for dinner here in your cabin."

"Oh, that will be fun and I only hope they have a better menu than last night."

"I have done my best. But short of seeking out the cook, who I am sure will be too busy to see me, I have left it in the hands of the Purser."

"Are we going straight to Rome?" Sacia asked him.

"I think we stop at one place on the way and then we leave this ship at the Port of Ostia and hire a carriage to take us to the City."

"Oh, I was wondering about that, Nico."

"Now you can stop worrying and enjoy yourself."

"I am enjoying myself so much because I am with you and because it is all so thrilling," Sacia sighed. "But I would be scared if I was alone on a ship like this."

Even as she spoke there was a loud burst of raucous laughter overhead and then yells and cries.

"I wonder what they are doing," Sacia asked.

"Leave them alone. We must try to ignore them, although I doubt if it will be easy to sleep if they are as noisy as this all night."

"Surely they will go to their cabins?"

"You heard what they told us when we came on board. We have the last cabins. This lot will either sleep on deck if it is not too cold or in the corridors."

Sacia looked rather apprehensive.

"It's all right, Sacia, I am here beside you. But as I have already said you must stay in your own cabin."

They were served dinner which the Prince thought was only just edible. There was, however, a bottle of wine that he considered just passable, although Sacia drank only one small glass.

As they began to go to bed the trouble started.

They could now hear more noise and commotion and the Prince gathered that the youths who could not have a cabin were given rough mattresses to sleep on.

There was, he realised, violent contention raging among them. This was because some of the mattresses were better than others and quite a number of them were fighting for what they claimed were their rights.

102

"Undress," the Prince suggested to Sacia, "and get into bed. Then I will come back and talk to you."

Without asking any questions Sacia obeyed him.

He felt that no other woman would have been so amenable.

Then when he went to his cabin, he could hear the turmoil outside and it would not only make it difficult to sleep, but would be dangerous for anyone who came into contact with this drunken mob.

They were distinctly unsteady and their language was unpleasant and because the ship was now rolling a little they were unable to keep on their feet.

The Prince waited until he was quite certain that Sacia would be in bed and then he took the mattress off his own bunk and carried it quickly to her cabin.

"What are you doing? What is happening?" Sacia asked him.

She sat up in her bunk looking very attractive and the Prince realised that as she had no nightgown, she was wearing her petticoat.

She had loosened her hair and it was cascading onto her shoulders.

He thought as he looked at her from the door that no one could be lovelier or more exquisite.

There came a loud drunken shout behind him and he moved quickly into Sacia's cabin pushing his mattress in front of him and closing the door behind him.

"Why are you bringing your mattress in here?" she questioned.

"Because I am going to sleep here on the floor," he replied.

"Have they taken away your cabin, Nico?"

"No, not so far, though they might if they realise it is now empty. But I don't want you to be alone. I am sure you don't want a gang of youths coming in and trying to talk to you, even though they will undoubtedly admire you. Every woman on board this ship is at least thirty or forty years older than you."

"Of course they must not come in here. Can you lock the door?"

"I am going to lock it now for what it is worth. I have already examined the locks. Mine is so very fragile it would break if it is given a hard push and yours seems not much better."

"You will be very uncomfortable on the floor."

"But I will not be as worried as I would be if I was next door and you were having men piling into your cabin merely to stare at you!"

"Now you are really frightening me – "

"I have no wish to do so, Sacia, and I have with me something I will most certainly use if they intrude on us."

"What can it be?"

He pulled his revolver from his belt and put it down on his mattress.

"That will protect us both, particularly you, Sacia. Now go to sleep and try not to worry yourself about what is happening outside."

"I will worry about you being uncomfortable and I think it is wonderful of you to come here and protect me. Those men are so noisy and – they sound very rough."

She spoke a little nervously.

"Forget them!" urged the Prince. "And now I too am going to sleep."

He took off his coat and put it on the floor and then he lay down just as he was on the mattress.

"I think you are very very kind," Sacia murmured from the bed. "I now feel I am really safe and no longer frightened. I was a little when I heard the noise they were making, but I did not want to worry you."

The Prince smiled.

"I am always worried if you are in any danger," he said. "And it is my solemn duty to protect you until you are completely and absolutely safe."

"Thank you, thank you, Nico. Now I am going to say a special prayer that we will both be safe from those we are running away from."

The Prince did not answer and after waiting for a moment she then slipped down in the bunk, put her hands together and closed her eyes.

He could not hear her prayers and yet the Prince felt as if there was something indefinable and spiritual in the cabin that had not been there before.

CHAPTER FIVE

It must have been an hour later that the shouts and screams came closer.

It woke the Prince first and then he became aware that the young ruffians had come down the companionway leading to the cabins.

In fact he could now hear them smashing the cabin doors.

As Sacia woke abruptly they both heard the youths shouting,

"We want women. Women to dance. Women to play with. *Where are the women*!"

Their voices rang out down the corridor and next came the crash of another door being forced and a woman screamed.

The Prince rose to his feet.

"Get down in the bunk," he ordered Sacia, "and cover yourself up completely."

She quickly obeyed him.

She was now terrified, but she felt sure the Prince would protect her.

He was standing by the door listening as the noise and shouts came nearer and nearer.

As the youths reached them, he flung open the door and fired his revolver into the ceiling.

It made a resounding noise in the narrow corridor and for a brief second there was silence from the rioters.

"I will shoot the next man who breaks a door," the Prince yelled, his voice ringing out so that they could all hear him. "Go back on deck where you belong and don't come down here again."

As he finished speaking he fired a second shot into the air.

The youths turned.

In a blind panic they began running up the corridor falling over one another in their anxiety to escape.

It was as the last youth disappeared that the woman who had already been dragged out of bed called from her cabin which was near the companionway,

"Thank you, sir, thank you."

The door opposite the Prince also opened and the man in the cabin had obviously been petrified as to what might happen next.

He called out to the Prince,

"You are a hero, that's what you are. I was really scared until you sent them away."

"They will not return," the Prince asserted, "but if they do, I am in here and I will keep my promise and shoot anyone who assaults us."

The Prince closed the cabin door and turned round to see Sacia peeping out from under the bedclothes.

He could just make her out faintly in the moonlight streaming in through the porthole.

But he saw that she was looking very beautiful and the expression in her eyes was one of admiration.

"You were so wonderful," she sighed. "I was really terrified as those other women must have been."

"I don't think they will come back now, but if they do, I will definitely shoot one of them to teach the others how to behave."

"If you kill one, there will be a scandal – "

"I am not as stupid as that, Sacia. I will shoot him in the leg or the arm and incidentally, in case you question me, I am a very good shot!"

"I'm quite certain you are, Nico. You are good at everything and most of all at protecting *me*!"

The Prince locked the cabin door and walked a few feet to Sacia's bunk.

He sat down on it, thinking the moonlight behind her hair was the most beautiful sight he had ever seen.

As he looked at her he remembered that she was sleeping in her petticoat, because she had no nightgown, and there were just two soft satin ribbons over her bare shoulders.

Her petticoat was more *décolletée* than an evening dress should have been on such a young girl.

She put out both her hands towards him.

It was only with a Herculean effort that the Prince restrained himself from putting his arms around her.

"You are safe now," he reassured her soothingly, "and we must both go to sleep again. I cannot allow you to arrive in Rome tired and travel-worn."

Sacia laughed.

"It has been another adventure," she smiled, "and we have had so many I have almost lost count."

The Prince reflected that he would remember them for the rest of his life, but he did not say so.

Instead he declared,

"You have been very brave, Sacia, and I can only say again you are a perfect companion. Now I am going to go to sleep."

He walked back to his mattress, thinking that never in his life had he been in such a series of situations.

Yet perhaps it was Sacia herself who made him do exactly the right thing every time – without pushing herself forward as other women would have done.

As he lay down Sacia sighed,

"You see my prayers were answered. I asked God and Aphrodite for help. It was they who told you to come to Venice to save me. I am now certain that they made you think how useful your revolver might be before you ran away."

"I am delighted you give them credit," the Prince replied, "but I would like to take a little of it for myself!"

"Of course you know you are wonderful," she said, "but you must be tired of hearing me say so."

"Go to sleep, Sacia. I suggest we leave this ship as soon as possible, but I am not letting you out of this cabin until those rampaging youths have gone ashore."

"I thought, as in all good adventure stories, I would perhaps end up being taken prisoner. I assure you I am content to be *your* prisoner even though I would prefer a more comfortable prison!"

"Is the bed very hard?" the Prince asked.

"It is rather like lying down on a cobbled yard, not that I have ever lain on one, but if we are together much longer, I am sure I will!"

"You never know your luck," the Prince replied.

They both laughed and then Sacia added,

"We really must sleep. Goodnight and thank you and God bless you, Nico. I never knew a man could be as magnificent as you are."

The Prince could not think of an answer.

A little later he was aware that Sacia was asleep and as he listened the noise from above appeared to have diminished considerably.

He supposed that the youths were either too drunk even to scream or had fallen asleep from sheer exhaustion.

He closed his eyes and although he expected to lie awake on the floor, he slept peacefully.

*

When morning came, it was Sacia who awoke first.

For a moment she could not think where she was and then the traumas of the previous night came rushing back into her mind.

The cabin was bright with the early morning sun and she could see the Prince lying on the floor and he was still fast asleep.

He must have turned towards her during the night, as when she last saw him she had been aware that although the door was locked, he was lying facing it still with his revolver was in his hand.

Now she could see quite clearly that this hand was empty and the revolver was beside him on the mattress.

She had not seen him asleep before and she thought he looked very much younger but a little vulnerable.

'He is protecting me,' she said to herself, 'but he should be protected too from those he is running away from.'

She thought that if they caught up with him, he may be in trouble and there would be no one to help him.

She wondered if she should suggest staying with him instead of going to her teacher and then she felt that if Nico wanted her to continue travelling with her he would say so.

'I must not push myself forward,' she decided, 'but when he has gone I will miss him very much.'

How different life would be if she just worked, as she had already suggested, with her previous teacher and it was a task she was sure she could do well.

She was also certain that there would be plenty of pupils to learn the many studies she was proficient in, most of all Greek – but it would not be the same as being with Nico and wondering what adventure might happen next.

'It has been so enthralling and maybe one day I will write it all down in a book,' she mused. 'But people will find it hard to believe.'

Then she wondered what her life would be like in the future.

It was one thing going to her previous teacher for help and safety, but it was quite another to contemplate spending the rest of her life teaching children and perhaps rather stupid young girls.

'I want to feel free. I want to roam the country. I want to be on a horse with Nico.'

It all swept over her.

She felt a pressing desire to jump out of bed, lie down beside him and beg him to take her with him.

Then she knew that would be an almost wicked thing for her to do. If he wanted her with him, he would ask her.

But if she forced herself upon him he would be in an uncomfortable position as he would either have to tell her he did not want her or, because he was so kind, he would pretend he did.

That would be unendurable and she would know instinctively as soon as he agreed.

Yet she could not help feeling that she was crying out to him to allow her to stay and be together with him.

Almost as if she called him aloud, she heard him stir and she lay back quickly in the bunk and shut her eyes.

She was acutely aware that Nico was near her.

Then, so silently she hardly heard him, he opened the door and went out locking it on the outside.

She heard him go to his own cabin next door and she thought he was washing himself and changing his shirt.

She had noticed that he had changed his shirt every day since they left Venice and she had wanted to ask if he would like her to wash one for him, but she had been too shy to suggest it.

Perhaps when they were staying with the Duca the servant who had valeted him would have had one washed and pressed for the following morning.

'I want to do things for him,' Sacia thought, 'but it would seem too intimate to suggest it. And I will have no chance of doing so anyway in the future.'

In his cabin the Prince washed and put on a clean shirt as Sacia was expecting him to do. He realised it was the last clean one in his possession.

He thought that when he left Sacia with her teacher, he might stay the night in a good hotel and they would wash his shirts and press his clothes before he moved on.

Then he asked himself where he should go once he had handed Sacia over to her teacher and safety.

He had of course a large number of acquaintances in Rome, but he had no wish to contact them at present.

He would have to explain why he was travelling without an equerry or a valet, or, as was usual when he visited Rome, with a bodyguard.

'Even when I lose Sacia,' he told himself, 'I can still pretend to be an ordinary man. And I must ask myself, before I take a wrong step, what an ordinary man would do in my position at this moment.'

Then he laughed.

How could he possibly be an ordinary man when his country was awaiting his return and when he had badly offended one of his most distinguished neighbours by not marrying his tiresome daughter?

And when he had so enjoyed the most astonishing adventures that any man, however ordinary, could have possibly encountered.

'If I was wise,' he told himself, 'I would take Sacia to Greece and not to her teacher. It is a country I would love to visit again and I can imagine nothing more exciting than to be with her.'

Then he reflected that it would only make matters more complicated than they were already.

If he was really in love with Sacia and felt he could not live without her, the difficulties ahead were obviously insurmountable.

The Prime Minister and the Cabinet, as well as his relations, had begged him almost on their knees to marry, but their ideas of a suitable marriage for him were very different from his.

They craved security for Vienz and they could only see it all happening if he married the daughter of another Ruler – otherwise the future he and his country had to face might be a precarious one.

He had been told a thousand times already, often in a whisper and sometimes more officially, that there were rumours that Italy would be as much of a danger in the future as Austria had been in the past.

His was an ancient and most respected Principality, but countries striving to increase their power would not have any scruples.

'I suppose the answer is,' he told himself with a sigh, 'that I will have to return home and find someone like Princess Marziale and pray to Heaven she is not in love with another man when she marries me!'

The mere thought of it made him feel that having run away he wanted to go on running.

These thoughts were all in his mind until he was ready to go up on deck and see what was happening.

By now they should be not too far away from their destination.

He went up the companionway and saw that the youths, exhausted by drink and rampaging, were asleep on deck – some of them had blankets, others were sleeping where they had fallen.

He turned towards the bridge and found the Captain of the ship.

"Are you all right?" the Captain asked, seeing the Prince looking distinguished amongst the riff-raff lying on the deck.

The Prince climbed up to the bridge.

"I know," the Captain began, "I must be grateful to you for stopping them doing more damage last night. I heard your shots ring out and was told that you prevented them from breaking into any more cabins."

"They did a little damage," the Prince replied, "but not as much as they might have done."

"Well, thank you, sir, and thank God we get rid of that lot in an hour's time."

"In Ostia?" the Prince asked in surprise.

"No, in Civitavecchia. It is where they have come from. They are a rough lot, but I have never known them quite as bad as they were last night."

"Too much alcohol," the Prince remarked.

"I realised that when it was too late and of course you will not be surprised to hear they drank more than they paid for. Another time the wine-store will be locked when they come aboard."

"I doubt if locks will prevent them from breaking in and stealing it. I suggest you take less on board in future."

The Captain laughed.

"I have put up with them on two other trips, but this has been easily the worst."

They were now moving into the harbour.

"I and my sister will stay below, Captain, until after they have disembarked. Then I hope for a good breakfast."

"I will see to it, sir, and I agree you should remain in your cabins until the ruffians have departed."

The Captain smiled as he left him and went below.

The Prince knocked on Sacia's cabin door.

When she asked a little nervously, "who is it?", he turned the key and walked in.

"You will be glad to hear, Sacia, our unwelcome guests are disembarking immediately. Then we go on to Ostia, the Port for Rome."

When he had entered the cabin, Sacia was sitting on her bunk gazing out of the porthole.

She was wearing the dress she had bought from the housekeeper and he thought she was looking entrancingly pretty.

"We will have breakfast together as soon as they have gone."

"That will be lovely," Sacia smiled.

Even as she spoke they were both aware that the ship was moving into the harbour.

There was the noise of chattering and shouts from above and this meant that the youths were awake and were signalling their arrival in their usual noisy manner.

The Prince sat down on the bunk.

"Tonight at least, Sacia, you will be able to sleep without being afraid."

"But also without anyone like you to protect me."

"You will not need it in Rome. I am sure there will always be someone to look after you there."

"But not in the same way as you have done," Sacia persisted. "And it is something I will never forget."

"I will not forget it too – "

Their eyes met and for a moment it was impossible for either of them to move.

Then, almost harshly, because he was afraid of his own feelings, the Prince stood up and walked across the cabin.

"I am going up above," he said, "to see what is happening. You are to stay here until I come back."

He did not look back and Sacia watched him until the door closed and she heard him turn the key in the lock.

'I just don't want to leave him, God,' she prayed. 'Please provide some reason for us to stay together a little longer and I will be *so* happy. I feel sure I can make him happy too.'

As she finished praying she was very close to tears.

She put her hands over her eyes, knowing that she must not cry in front of Nico.

She must be brave until he had finally left her.

He seemed to be away a long time, but it was only because some of the youths were still suffering from the effects of too much drink. They were so unsteady when they were finally woken up that their friends had to carry them off the ship.

Only as the last of them struggled ashore did the Captain quickly sail out of the harbour.

The Prince, who had been standing near the bridge, went below to join Sacia again.

She jumped to her feet as soon as he appeared.

"Have they all gone?" she asked him breathlessly.

"Every one of them. Now I hope they will give us something substantial to eat because I am really hungry."

"I doubt if it will be very exciting. But I will be content with a cup of good strong coffee."

"We have had every kind of food since we set out on our adventure," added the Prince, "and it will not be hard to remember the good as there has been so little of it!"

Sacia laughed.

118

"Like everything else, it was not exactly what we expected, but that is what makes an adventure different from all one does every day and every night."

"You always give me the right answer, Sacia, and I cannot imagine what it will be like when we are apart."

"I was just thinking the same," Sacia said in a low voice.

She thought, as he did not answer, that he had not heard her and she told herself she must be very careful not to reveal how much she minded losing him.

It was only a short way from Civitavecchia to the Port of Ostia at the mouth of the Tiber.

There was just enough time to eat their breakfast and then they disembarked and the Prince hired a carriage to take them the thirteen miles to Rome.

Sacia prevented herself from telling him how sad she was that their adventures were now at an end.

'He has no idea who I am and yet the only way he would expect me to behave is like a lady,' she told herself. 'Like those who were taken to the guillotine, I must hold my head high and not show that I am both apprehensive and miserable at losing him.'

*

As they approached Rome, the Prince was aware in the distance of many familiar sights – the Seven Hills, the many bridges, the domes, the towers and the beauty of the Eternal City that had always delighted him ever since he was a child.

He sensed that Sacia was feeling the same.

As they drew nearer to the Ponte Palatino, he took her hand in his.

"You must promise me, Sacia, that you will look after yourself when I leave you and if you are in trouble, I feel somehow as if I will hear your cry to me."

He felt Sacia's fingers tremble and went on,

"In some mysterious way, perhaps by the kindness of Aphrodite, I will sense what you are feeling and come instantly to your rescue."

"Do you really believe that?" Sacia asked him.

"Of course I do. I saved your life in the first place by a miracle and everything that has happened since we have been together has made it clear that we feel the same and think the same. Therefore if ever you need me again, I will come at once and save you."

He was speaking with a deep sincerity she could not doubt.

It flashed through her mind it would be so much easier if they did not have to part, but she knew it was something she must not say.

"I feel – sure," she said a little unsteadily, "I will be safe with my teacher. But, as you say, perhaps in the same way as you saved my life once – you will save me again."

The Prince smiled at her.

"You are very beautiful. You must remember that beautiful women are always in danger from men."

Sacia thought of the young ruffians who had been breaking up the ship last night and shivered.

"Forget them! But if you go on that sort of ship again, make certain you are chaperoned and be very careful always to lock yourself in your cabin."

"I will do it because you have told me to, Nico."

"Now how far is your teacher's house from here?" he asked. "As it is a lovely warm day, I would rather like to stretch my legs."

"We can easily walk. I know exactly where it is from here. If we go along the river, it is always interesting in the morning to see the barges filled with goods and I love crossing the bridges."

"What woman could resist the shops on them," the Prince added teasingly.

"I will need to visit plenty of shops if I am to stay in Rome."

"I feel sure and I did not have a chance of giving you anything except that one dress from the housekeeper. I assure you that if I had seen any dress shops on our way, I would at least have bought you a nightgown."

Sacia looked at him and then she realised he must have noticed last night that she had been sleeping in her petticoat as she had done ever since she ran away.

She blushed and it made her look even lovelier than ever.

With a brave gesture she replied,

"You are fortunate to be rid of me before I have to buy myself not just nightgowns but a whole new wardrobe. In fact I will have to work hard to pay back my teacher."

"Supposing she will not have you?"

It had not occurred to him before and he realised that the possibility had not occurred to Sacia either.

"I never thought of it," she said. "She may already have an assistant and will not need another one. Although I think she was fond of me, I was just her pupil and she was paid for teaching me."

She was obviously upset by the suggestion and the Prince added quickly,

"I tell you what we will do. As you don't want to tell her that you have been with me, I will not come in with you."

Sacia nodded as she thought this was sensible.

"Instead I will wait in the road outside," the Prince continued. "If your teacher says she does not want you or it is impossible for her to hide you, then you must come back to me and we will start all over again."

"Do you really mean that, Nico? I know I am being a nuisance and a burden which I hate to be. It was very stupid of me to be so certain that she would welcome me."

"There has been no harm done. After all we had to make for this part of Italy, because there was no possibility of going elsewhere. If we continue our journey together, that is just fate and we *must* accept it."

"We cannot go on running for ever," she sighed, "but I would be overwhelmingly grateful if you could find me somewhere safe – before you leave me."

She stumbled over the last words.

Once again when their eyes met it was difficult to look away.

"Now come along, Sacia. We are talking too much and doing too little."

The Prince paid off the carriage and they started to walk up the road and he noticed that Sacia was deliberately not hurrying.

He wondered if he should ask her to stay with him a little longer and they might have a really good luncheon in one of the restaurants he remembered only too well.

Then he told himself it would be dangerous.

It was likely that someone would recognise him and apart from friends, there were several of his relatives who lived just outside the City.

They would of course often be shopping or visiting friends in Rome itself, but he thought it was unlikely they would be about this early in the morning.

He would be wise, however, when he had deposited Sacia with her teacher to return to Ostia and board one of the many vessels that were always loading or unloading at the mouth of the Tiber.

If he decided to stay away for longer and give Ruta more time to announce his marriage to Princess Marziale, he could visit Greece, which he had always loved and then, if he still had no desire to return home, he could move across the Mediterranean to Alexandria.

'The world is my oyster,' he thought to himself. 'Why should I be compelled to go home until I am ready to do so?'

"You are feeling defiant," Sacia said unexpectedly. "Why?"

"Are you reading my thoughts again or are you just instinctively conscious that is what I am feeling?"

"I think it is a mixture of both, Nico, but I do know what you are feeling. You are still rebelling at fate, as you were when we first met, or whatever is threatening you."

"I was indeed being threatened when I ran away," he admitted, "and the same was happening to you. That is why we have been so happy together and found an affinity that others would not have had."

"Of course that is the reason. That is why I am even more determined not to be forced into marriage."

"I am saying the same thing to myself. I only hope I will be strong enough, as you have been, to fight off those who have very different ideas as to what we should do and what is our duty."

He spoke the last words almost as if he spat them out and then Sacia added softly,

"I know you are so strong and so brave that no one could ever make you do anything you don't want to do. We must pray and pray very hard that what you need and what you are seeking is yours when you most desire it."

"I wonder if that is possible in this world. It is the happy ending that only ever happens in books or in Heaven which, at the moment, you and I do not inhabit!"

"But we can go on hoping, and, as I have already said, praying that we will both find all we seek."

The Prince smiled and then they realised there were more pedestrians on the pavement and it was difficult to talk and move forward at the same time.

He was still carrying his bag in one hand and with the other he guided Sacia through the throng of people as best he could although impeded by his bag.

They swore as he bumped into them and not always under their breath.

"We cross the river here," Sacia told him.

They walked onto the Ponte Sisto and she could not resist stopping at some of the shops.

There was one which sold the most beautiful coral jewellery and the Prince longed to go in and buy her some.

He thought that the pink against her skin would be lovely, but he felt it would be wrong as they were parting.

Anyway there was no point in making a further tie between them now that they were about to separate.

"You can see how beautiful the coral is," Sacia was saying, "when it is polished and made into jewellery. I have stopped at this shop before and I am sure you have noticed in another one they sell antique jewels."

She gave a little laugh.

"I have sometimes thought if one buys and wears old jewellery one might absorb its history which perhaps could have been violent."

The Prince grimaced.

"I think we have had enough of that to last us for a lifetime."

"I believe you will always be involved in fighting for what is good against what is bad, Nico. If you were a King, you would defend your country against the enemy even if you died doing so."

The Prince thought that once again she was being clairvoyant. She was perhaps seeing him fight for Vienz to keep it independent.

"Actually," Sacia continued, "that will not happen to you. I have a feeling, although I may be wrong, that you are very powerful. You will always have people following you because you fight for what is just and right."

"I cannot imagine why you are thinking that at this particular moment, Sacia, and actually I have no wish, now you are leaving me, to fight anyone."

"It is just that I was seeing you almost as if I was looking into a crystal," Sacia replied in a dreamy voice. "But, as I have said, you will not die, but you will help a great many people as you have helped me."

Again she was speaking almost as if she was in a clairvoyant trance and because it made him uncomfortable he tried to change the subject,

"I only hope that the food is better and the beds are softer than we have endured on this trip."

Sacia laughed as he meant her to do.

"I cannot see it happening and if you are a soldier, as I believe you are, you may have to sleep on the hard ground."

"Now you are scaring me," the Prince protested. "And where do we go from here."

He saw the sudden sadness in Sacia's eyes and he felt as he had before that he was being cruel in leaving her.

Yet how could they go on for ever wandering over the world?

He wanted, more than he had ever wanted anything in his whole life, to kiss her – to hold her close against him and tell her he loved her.

He now knew that he loved her with all his heart and soul, but it was hopeless for him to say so.

How could he marry a girl who had run away from home? Someone he knew absolutely nothing about except that she was extremely beautiful and utterly adorable.

Sacia was walking beside him as they moved off the bridge and onto the road on the other side of the river.

She had ceased to talk and was no longer looking at him, but he recognised, as he now knew her every different mood, that she was upset and distressed.

He longed to comfort her.

Yet he could only do so by saying they could stay together, that they could go on adventuring and would still remain anonymous not only to the world but to each other.

How could he say it?

And just how could he more or less take her into his possession without offering her marriage?

Because he loved her so much he would not offer her anything else.

He would not be a man if he had not thought of it a million times.

Yet because she was obviously a lady and because he would not treat her as if she was just a *cocotte*, he had protected her against other men and indeed himself.

'It has been a dream that can never come true,' he thought as they turned off the bridge into a wide road.

They only went a short way when Sacia paused.

"This is where my teacher lives. Her house is only halfway down this road."

She now walked a little slower and he knew it was because she was fighting against the moment when they were forced to say goodbye.

They would never see each other again.

"Now what I will do," the Prince insisted, "is stand in the doorway of one of these houses. This one looks as if it is empty and I will stay here while you see your teacher. If she agrees to have you, then I will go away. If not, you can come back and join me."

They had now stopped walking.

A hired carriage passed, otherwise there appeared to be no one on the street.

"Must – we really – say goodbye?" Sacia asked.

Her voice broke on the words.

"I am afraid so," the Prince answered. "All good things have to come to an end and this adventure of yours and mine has been wonderful and very precious to me."

"And very precious to me too," sighed Sacia.

They looked at each other.

The Prince made no movement to touch her.

He felt if he did so, it would be difficult to control himself.

For a moment there were no words.

Neither of them could say what they were feeling or what they were thinking.

Then with what the Prince sensed was an almost superhuman effort, Sacia turned round.

She knew there was nothing she could say and the words would now be completely ineffectual anyway.

She stepped from the doorway of the empty house and walked slowly towards her teacher's house.

The Prince's eyes followed her.

Suddenly he saw her stop abruptly.

He wondered why.

Then he saw ahead down the road the hired carriage that had passed them had stopped at one of the houses.

He thought as Sacia was standing still it must be the house of her teacher.

Then a man stepped out with a gesture that told the coachman to wait for him and walked up to the door.

Sacia, who had been standing absolutely still as if frozen into immobility, turned round.

Then she ran back towards the Prince.

One glance at the expression on her face told him that something was wrong.

She flung herself against him and his arms went round her.

"Hide me! Hide me!" she gasped. "That is one of Papa's men."

CHAPTER SIX

The Prince held Sacia close in his arms.

Then he turned her swiftly round so that he had his back to the road while she was against the door.

As he felt her trembling, his lips came down on hers and held her captive.

He kissed her demandingly, possessively and then passionately as if he would never let her go.

For a moment she was surprised into immobility and then her whole body seemed to melt into his.

Sacia felt as if his kisses carried her up into the sky.

How long he kissed her and went on kissing her, the Prince had no idea.

He only knew that something had broken within him and he could not live without her.

He had steeled himself to let her go, but now he knew she was his and nothing must ever separate them.

Finally, after what seemed an extremely long time, he raised his head.

"My darling, my sweet," he murmured in a voice that did not sound like his own. "How can I love you so much? How can I let you leave me?"

"I love you too. I *do* love you," Sacia exclaimed. "I thought you no longer wanted me."

"Of course I want you, and what is more, Sacia, I will never again let you leave me – *ever*."

Then, as if he remembered the reason why she had run back to him, he glanced over his shoulder.

The carriage was still standing outside her teacher's house halfway down the street.

"It was one of – Papa's men – I saw go in," Sacia faltered. "If he sees me – he will recognise me at once."

"He will not see you," the Prince asserted firmly as he looked again at the carriage.

"We are much safer here than if we try to move. Just peep over my shoulder and tell me when he comes out. He must not see me either."

The Prince was thinking that, if the man had come from Venice, he might know him and someone might even have seen Sacia going away in the gondola with him.

Whatever the situation one fact was obvious.

Neither of them must be seen by the man who was now visiting Sacia's teacher.

He pushed Sacia a little further back against the closed door and held her as close to him as he could.

She was no longer trembling.

He now realised that the wonder of their kisses had swept away her fear.

"I love you, my darling," the Prince said in a low voice, "and now at last I can tell you so."

"I thought that you would never love me," Sacia whispered. "But I prayed every night that you would love me enough – to keep me with you."

"I cannot think how I was so foolish as to think I could let you go, but I was actually thinking of you rather than myself."

"And I was thinking of you, Nico. I have thought of nothing else these wonderful days when we have been together."

"There will be many more of them – "

He was thinking that, however much it might upset his Cabinet, his country and family he would never give her up.

He was just about to say so when she gave a start and without looking round he realised that the man must have come out of her teacher's house.

"What is happening?" he asked.

"He is getting into – the carriage," Sacia whispered.

There was no chance of their voices carrying that distance, but the Prince realised that she whispered because her fear was back.

She was trembling again.

"You are quite safe, my darling one," he insisted.

"He may pass us," Sacia muttered.

She peeped over his shoulder and then gave a sigh of relief.

"He is driving off the other way – and not coming back."

"We will not move till the carriage is out of sight," the Prince said firmly. "Besides, my precious, I want to kiss you once more."

His lips found hers again and he thought nothing could be more perfect than her sweetness and innocence.

Then Sacia looked over his shoulder and sighed,

"The carriage has gone."

"Then we will leave in the opposite direction."

The Prince picked up the bag he had put down on the doorstep and then he looked carefully down the road to be quite certain that the carriage had not turned and come back.

The road was now empty except for a small child who came out of one of the houses with a dog on a lead.

"Now come along, Sacia. We have to leave Rome as quickly as possible."

He felt as he spoke that he had really been very stupid in bringing her here in the first place.

He might have guessed, if he had used his brain, that Sacia's father might send someone to interview the teacher where she had been educated.

In fact as he thought it over, he should have realised she would be more willing to hide her than friends would be as they would feel they owed her father an obligation rather than his daughter.

The Prince was reproaching himself as they walked quickly back into the road that led to the bridge.

Then coming towards them he could see a Hackney carriage and that it was unoccupied.

He waved to it.

He realised as he did so that because he had moved so quickly Sacia had started nervously.

"A carriage!" the Prince said unnecessarily as the man pulled in his horses. "And now we have a number of things to do quickly. First is to find you some clothes."

"Clothes!" Sacia cried in amazement. "But why?"

"Because my darling one, we are now setting off on a new adventure and this time we are going on a proper ship. Rome is too dangerous for us and the sooner we get away from Italy the better."

"Of course you are right, Nico. And it was silly of me to think of coming here in the first place."

"It was stupid of me not to realise you might be walking directly into your father's hands."

The carriage stopped opposite them and the Prince opened the door and helped Sacia into it.

Then he called to the driver,

"Take us to a shop in one of the main streets which has the best selection of women's clothes."

The coachman scratched his head before he replied,

"There be a great number of smart shops in Rome, sir."

"Well you chose what you think is the best, but we are in a hurry, so don't take us too far."

He climbed into the carriage and as he shut the door Sacia asked,

"Are you going to buy me something to wear?"

"I could not be so mean as to deprive you of even a nightgown, my darling, but we have to be clever about this and you will have to let me choose for you. It would be dangerous for you to go into the shop yourself."

"Yes, of course."

"Now please unpack the dress you were wearing when you jumped out of the window in Venice."

She did not argue with him which he thought any other woman might have done and nor did she ask a lot of questions.

She obeyed him and pulled the dress out of his bag and the Prince smoothed it out on the seat beside him.

Then he put his arms round Sacia again.

"Now listen and this is very important. I am going in to buy you what clothes I can, and what I deem essential for the journey ahead of us."

She was looking up at him her, eyes very wide.

"Now while I am in the shop," the Prince went on, "you are in danger, because someone passing might look into the carriage and recognise you."

"I realise that, so I must hide my face."

"That might look suspicious. What I suggest you do is take my handkerchief, as you don't have one of your own and hold it to your nose as if you had a cold. Also sit as far back in the carriage as possible."

"But your beautiful hair might give you away, so put one of my other handkerchiefs over your head. But make it look attractive and not just a handkerchief."

Sacia laughed.

"You must think I am very silly."

"I think you are glorious, very beautiful and above all mine!"

He kissed her again so that there was no chance of her answering.

Then almost at once the carriage stopped outside what appeared to be a large and expensive shop.

"Now sit in the corner and don't forget you have a bad cold."

The Prince opened the door.

He jumped out of the carriage before the coachman could climb down from the box.

"My sister is not well as we had a rough passage on a ship last night. She also had her luggage stolen when she was on board. I therefore need to buy her some clothes, so I might be quite a while in the shop."

The coachman was listening intently as he went on,

"Look after her for me, as she is not well enough for me to take her to a friend's house."

The coachman nodded as if he understood.

Then he fastened his reins and very slowly came down from the box and stood in front of the carriage as if to protect Sacia from any intrusion.

The Prince hurried into the shop to see that it sold almost every article of clothing a woman might desire.

"I wish to speak to the manager," he said in a voice that indicated he was a gentleman of some consequence.

It was fortunate that the manager was not far away.

He came up and the Prince announced grandly,

"I am Count Teodoro and I am in a great hurry as I have to catch a ship at Porto Ostia. My sister, who is with me, has had her luggage stolen and now requires urgently everything she might need for a voyage to Greece."

He saw that the manager's eyes were on him.

"We have people waiting for us there as soon as we arrive, but all she has now is what she stands up in."

"I quite understand, sir, it is a terrible disaster!" the Manager exclaimed.

"This is the dress she has been wearing, which is the only article I have been able to replace in a hurry. As she is feeling ill after the shock of the robbery, she has left it to me to ask you to provide her with three day dresses the same size as this dress, two evening gowns and everything a woman requires underneath."

The manager gave an audible gasp and beckoned to two vendeuses.

As it was still fairly early in the morning they were not busy and had been admiring the Prince.

The manager rapidly repeated what the Prince had told him. He handed one woman the dress, while the other hurried to another department. The Prince guessed she was going to find nightgowns, petticoats and all the other items that Sacia would require.

"As my sister is young and attractive," he added, "I think she would like a pink, a blue and a white dress for the day and something fashionable to wear in the evening, also in pale colours as she is only just eighteen."

"I understand, sir," the manager nearly genuflected.

The vendeuse with Sacia's dress in her hand went to her department.

"Do you require hats and shoes?" the manager then enquired.

The Prince thought for a moment.

"Hats certainly, but remember they are for a young girl, so they must be pretty and if possible trimmed with flowers."

The manager smiled.

"We have a reputation in Rome," he boasted, "for making even the plainest girl look lovely when she wears our hats and our gowns."

"Then I must certainly congratulate our coachman on bringing me here. I will just ask my sister what size of shoes she takes."

He walked across the pavement and he could see, before realising he was coming, that Sacia was obeying his instructions.

She was sitting in the far corner of the carriage and holding one handkerchief to her nose and another arranged so that it covered the front of her hair.

As the Prince opened the door, she peeped over the handkerchief and exclaimed,

"You cannot have done all the shopping already!"

"I have ordered it all, Sacia, but I had forgotten that you need shoes. Give me one of yours and I will buy you three pairs, one of which will be comfortable for walking. There is always so much walking to do in Greece."

"Is that where we are going?" cried Sacia.

He heard the excitement in her voice.

"If we can locate a ship to carry us, that is where I really want to take you, but don't look so happy! You are supposed to be ill!"

Sacia giggled and held out one of her feet and he took the shoe off it and hurried back into the shop.

While he had been away, the vendeuse had brought three day dresses for his approval.

One was white, which was what he had asked for, one was the soft blue of the sky and the third a rather vivid pink.

"The pink is too harsh," the Prince commented.

"That is just what I thought," the manager replied, "but it is made by a Master hand and we thought you might prefer it."

"But it is a little fussy for a young girl."

He thought as he spoke how in Paris he had often helped chose a gown. It would have been for one of the sophisticated women with whom he had enjoyed a fiery but short *affaire-de-coeur*.

They had always wanted him to buy not only the most expensive gown but the most seductive and that was *not* what he wanted for Sacia.

The vendeuse brought another dress in pink and white and he just knew that Sacia would look very young and completely adorable in it.

"I will take those three," he said, "and what about the evening gowns?"

139

Although more elegant, they were suitable for a young girl and he selected one warmly lined, again in a blue but a deeper blue than the dress.

The Prince then inspected the shoes that had been brought from the shoe department and chose a soft flexible pair for Sacia to wear on deck and a pair of strong walking shoes.

He recalled that, unlike other women, Sacia had never complained when walking across the fields towards the Castle even though her shoes were obviously intended only for a parquet floor or an expensively carpeted one.

The vendeuse then returned with a large armful of underclothes and she wanted to display exactly what she had chosen, but the Prince waved her on one side.

"I trust you have not forgotten anything," he said, "as my poor sister has only the clothes she is wearing."

The manager produced two rather expensive cases for the clothes and a hat-box for the hats.

The Prince looked at them quickly and was certain she would look lovely in all of them and then he called for the bill.

Actually the bill when it came was not as heavy as the Prince had expected, but he was glad that when he ran away from the Palace, he had been sensible enough to take a very large sum of money from the safe in his bedroom.

Actually they had spent very little of it so far on their adventurous journey and he thought, if they were as economical as they had been so far, they would be able to stay away for at least a year.

Then he rebuked himself for playing truant.

Sooner rather than later, however difficult it might be, he had to return, but he did not wish to think about it at this moment.

He thanked the manager profusely for his attention and complimented the vendeuses so that they smiled and blushed.

Then he walked out of the shop with the manager and a porter carrying the two cases and the hat-box and they were placed at the back of the Hackney carriage.

The Prince tipped the porter and shook the manager by the hand.

"I am extremely grateful to you and although this is my first visit to your shop, it will not be my last."

"We will only be too eager to serve you, sir. May I wish you *bon voyage*, and I am sure the young lady will be pleased with the clothes you have chosen for her."

He then told the coachman to drive as quickly as he could to the Ponte Palatino.

Only when they were out of sight of the shop did Sacia take the handkerchief away from her nose.

"Have you bought me some lovely clothes?" she asked him.

"None of them as lovely as you, Sacia, but they will be a frame for your beauty and I was thinking of that when I chose them."

"You say such wonderful words to me, Nico, as I felt you would if you love me a little."

141

"I love you a great deal more than that, as I will tell you when you have the time to listen."

Sacia chuckled.

"I will always listen to you, but I am finding it hard to believe this is happening and I am not dreaming again."

"Have you dreamt of me before?" the Prince asked.

"Of course I have. I have dreamt of you almost every night and was afraid when I woke up you might have become bored with me and disappeared."

"Did you really think that I would do anything so absurd?"

He saw the question in her eyes and added,

"I was letting you go for refuge to your teacher because I thought that was best for you."

"If I had gone a little earlier or a little later it would have been disastrous," Sacia said in a frightened voice. "I would have had to go back to Papa who would have been very angry with me."

There was that worried note back in her voice and it told the Prince that it would be a mistake to talk any more about it.

"Now what we have to plan," he said, "is how to spirit you on board a ship without you being in any way noticeable. I suppose, now that I think of it, I should have brought you one of the hats to put on now."

"Perhaps we should take one out of the hat-box."

"The one thing we don't want to do is for you look unusual in any way."

142

"You think of everything so brilliantly, Nico. No one else could have been as clever as you have been ever since I fell out of the window and into your gondola."

"We must not pat ourselves on the back until we arrive safely at our destination. We must be very careful of every step we take until there is no chance of either of us seeing anyone we know or being recognised."

It was only a short distance to the Ponte Palatino and as the carriage stopped, the Prince could see that down on the river several barges were unloading passengers.

They had come from the Antico Porto and then he saw that there were smaller boats for visitors to be ferried up or down the river at their convenience.

When he thought of it, he remembered years ago on his first visit as a young boy his father had always hired one, as he said he disliked being crushed by a lot of noisy people – in fact he preferred more than anything else to travel in silence.

"Are we now going in a barge?" Sacia asked.

"We are going to have a barge to ourselves, so stay here and again keep as inconspicuous as possible until I come back."

He jumped out of the carriage, told the coachman to wait and went down the steps to the river.

It did not take him long to find there were quite a number of private barges for hire and he chose one that was larger and looked more solidly built than the others.

He told the boatman that he wished to go down to the Port of Ostia and the Prince knew he was delighted as it

143

was a more expensive trip than sailing down the river with sightseers.

The Prince went back to the carriage and paid the coachman giving him a tip that made him bow politely and wish them a happy journey.

He then unloaded their luggage.

Fortunately, as always at such places, there were a few boys ready to carry luggage or do anything else to earn them a few centesimi.

The Prince held back one case until the youths had gone off with the others and then he opened it and found as he remembered that there was a scarf on top of the dresses.

He shut the case up again and told the coachman to give it to another boy to take down to the river.

Then he opened the carriage door and handed the scarf to Sacia.

"That was clever of you," she exclaimed.

"Wrap it over your head and cover as much of your face as you can, then tie the ends round your neck."

Sacia obeyed him and did so very elegantly.

Then the Prince helped her out of the carriage.

As they both thanked the coachman, he guided her down the steps that led to the river below.

The barge was waiting for them.

The boys were delighted with the money the Prince gave them and as they moved off they cheered and waved.

The Prince acknowledged them by raising his hand and then he sat himself comfortably close to Sacia and put his arm round her.

The barge had a cover which he had told the man to raise.

It was really meant to be protection against rain, but he wanted to keep them from being seen by people on the banks of the river or from boats they were passing.

It did not take as long as he had expected to cover the thirteen miles to Ostia and it had fascinated the Prince when he was a boy when he was taught about this ancient Roman Port.

He thought now it was an appropriate beginning to their new adventure together and perhaps this would be the most significant one of them all.

He knew he could not let Sacia leave him again whoever she was or wherever she came from.

She was his.

He would keep her whatever the difficulties that might arise from either of their backgrounds.

'I love her,' the Prince mused. 'She is the one I was really looking for when I set out on this adventure. Now I have found her I will never be such a fool as to lose her.'

They talked very little as the barge sailed down the Tiber, but Sacia was feeling how wonderful it was to have the Prince's arm around her.

She knew in her heart when she gazed into his eyes that he loved her.

The Prince was aware that every time they looked at each other, Sacia's face was transformed into a beauty which was the perfection of love.

The love he had always longed for when he thought of the Goddess Aphrodite.

'She has sent me real love,' he told himself, 'and I must never ever lose it. She has brought me *the miracle of love*.'

Equally he could feel there was a menace hovering over his head.

Unless Sacia could in any way be of help to Vienz, he could visualise that every powerful force in his country would try to separate them.

It was something he could not say to Sacia, but her instinct told her that he was troubled.

At the same time his love for her was stronger than the troubles in his mind.

"You are not regretting that we are together again?" she whispered.

"I am thanking God," replied the Prince, "that He showed me before it was too late that I was a fool in letting you go. You are mine, Sacia, all mine, and whatever the future holds for us I will never give you up."

He spoke defiantly as if it was being demanded of him at that very moment.

"I feel that the Goddess Aphrodite is guiding us," Sacia sighed. "It cannot be just chance that I was saved with just a few seconds to spare from falling into the hands of my father's men. And it cannot be by chance that you had not turned away thinking I was safe with my teacher."

"You are absolutely right, my darling. Aphrodite has guided and helped us ever since you swung down from the window and into my gondola. How can we then be so ungrateful as to question the future?"

Sacia reckoned that was what he had been doing, but she did not say anything.

She now slipped her hand into his and moved just a little closer and she could feel his love flooding over her.

When they arrived at the Port of Ostia, the Prince lifted Sacia out of the boat and then he went to see which ships had arrived or were expected.

The first ship he saw, as soon as he walked into the harbour, he recognised as an English ship. It was not very large, but it was flying the Red Ensign and it looked like a pleasure cruiser that the English had recently introduced into the Mediterranean.

He felt again that Sacia was right and he had been guided towards this ship by Aphrodite.

He then stepped on board the ship and saw some of the passengers walking about the deck.

He realised they were people of a good class and bore no relation to the noisy rampageous youths they had travelled with yesterday.

He sought out the Purser who was a middle-aged man in uniform and he looked somewhat harassed.

"Will you tell me where you are going," the Prince asked him, "and if you have any accommodation vacant?"

147

He spoke English well with a faint foreign accent.

The Purser, who had not looked at him when he had stood outside his Office, turned round slowly as if he was bored by the question.

Seeing that the Prince was obviously a gentleman of distinction, he replied more politely than he would have otherwise,

"I have only three cabins left, sir. One which has just been vacated is our best first-class double cabin for a married couple. The others are two small cabins in second class."

As if the Prince was being prompted, he said,

"I will take your first-class cabin and I hope that you are going to Greece."

"We will be calling at Athens, sir. Then we are going on through the Greek Islands to Constantinople."

"I wish to leave you at Athens," said the Prince. "I will now fetch my wife and I will be grateful if you would send two porters for my luggage."

The Purser produced his book.

"May I have your name, sir?"

The Prince hesitated for a second and then told him,

"I am Count Nicolo Theodoro."

"We are delighted to have you on board, sir," the Purser added in a polite tone.

He pushed the book towards the Prince.

"Will you please sign your name here, sir."

The Prince signed the name he had given himself and then he walked to the barge with two porters following him.

Then he helped Sacia out of the barge and putting his arm around her he guided her up the gangway and onto the ship.

The Purser had already opened the cabin for them and the porters carried in their luggage.

It was as the Prince had expected, quite large with a double bed instead of a bunk, as was usual in English ships that carried distinguished passengers in their best cabins.

There was a bathroom with a shower opening out of it and there was every possible modern comfort in the way of a dressing table, cupboards, wardrobes and a fitted chest of drawers.

Sacia was wise enough not to say anything while the porters were bringing in their luggage.

When they were alone, she took the handkerchief away from her nose and pushed the scarf back from her hair.

"What a lovely cabin," she cried. "Is this for you or for me?"

The Prince glanced to see that the door was closed.

"We are on an English ship, my darling, and I think you may know that it is possible at sea and completely within the law for the Captain to marry his passengers."

Sacia stood very still.

She looked at the Prince wide-eyed.

"*What* are you saying to me?" she whispered.

"I am saying, my precious, that I am not going to lose you again nor can you lose me. We belong to each other and we both believe we have been brought together by the Goddess Aphrodite. So I am now asking you, if you love me enough, to become my wife."

For a moment Sacia just stared at him.

Then she gave a little cry and flung her arms round his neck.

"I love you, I love you, Nico, and I thought even though I prayed for it that you would never marry me. Oh, darling wonderful Nico, I want to be married to you and I would adore to be your wife. But do you really and truly want me?"

The Prince held her very close.

"Really and truly – and this is exactly what I have been seeking and why I set off on my adventure."

He kissed her at first very gently.

Then, when she thought he was going to take her high into the sky again, he gently set her free.

"Listen, my darling. If we are married, as I know that we can be once the ship is at sea, I want to spend our honeymoon in Greece and to think only of Aphrodite and the way she has helped us."

"That is what I want to do too," mumbled Sacia.

"I know therefore, because I want our honeymoon to be a very happy one, I don't want either of us to think of the future or of any problems that may lie ahead.

"We both know there may be difficulties now that we have embarked on this wonderful adventure. We have now found each other and the love we are both seeking."

"Oh, Nico, that is true absolutely true. I love you so incredibly much, but I never thought my prayers would be answered and that you would make me your wife."

"That is exactly what I intend to do. So let us enjoy ourselves as two people who have found the Divine love they have been searching for and leave the difficulties to come later."

"Of course we should do and it is just what I want myself. Explanations and speculations always make one miserable."

"That is what I think too," the Prince smiled.

"So we will just be Nico and Sacia as we have been ever since I fell into the gondola until we know we have to return home and tell our families the whole story."

She moved closer to the Prince as she sighed,

"But for the moment by God's mercy or perhaps by the magic of Aphrodite we will think only of ourselves and the love they have given us."

"I knew you would understand, Sacia."

He realised that once again he was running away.

Running away not only from telling Sacia who he was, but from learning that she came from some respected but ordinary Venetian family.

As there was no Royalty in Venice, she would not be accepted readily or eagerly as a Royal Princess and she could bring no advantage or security to Vienz.

He put his arms out to draw her closer still.

"I love you, I adore you, my darling Sacia, and that is the only subject we are going to think about until our honeymoon is over."

The Prince did not wait for Sacia to answer him.

He was kissing her until it was impossible for either of them to think of anything else but the glory and mystery of their love for each other.

*

The ship sailed an hour later.

When they had left the harbour and were moving slowly down the coast towards Sicily, the Prince left Sacia.

He learnt from a Steward that as the ship was now full, they were not stopping at Naples.

The Prince had to ask the Purser if he could see the Captain and he realised that it was only his air of dignity and his title that eventually made it possible. It was clearly the Purser's job to protect the Captain from the passengers.

Finally after quite a wait the Prince found himself speaking with the Captain on the bridge.

The ship was moving smoothly over a quiet sea and he was interested to see it boasted every new and modern improvement.

"You wanted to see me," the Captain said a little aggressively.

He found it tiresome when passengers wanted to speak to him as soon as they were out of Port.

"I would be most grateful, Captain," the Prince now began, "if you will marry me and the lady who is with me whilst we are at sea."

He saw surprise on the Captain's face and went on,

"I don't need to tell you that we have had to run away from our respective families who have different ideas of who we should marry, but, as we are overwhelmingly in love with each other, we knew the only action we can take is to make our marriage a *fait accompli* so that they could no longer quarrel over us."

There was a moment's silence and then the Captain threw back his head and laughed.

"I can quite understand, Count Theodoro, that you have been brave enough to take fate into your own hands. Of course I will marry you and will be delighted to do so. I imagine that you will find Greece the perfect place for a honeymoon."

"I must admit I had no idea an Englishman could be so understanding!" the Prince exclaimed.

The Captain laughed again.

"I will marry you in exactly an hour's time, Count. As you are in our best cabin, I will perform the wedding ceremony there for you."

"I am so grateful to you, Captain, and I would like, as long as it is not published, to have the best wishes of the crew. But I want the fact we are married to be kept secret from the passengers. They would undoubtedly try to give us their good wishes, which would be embarrassing. But if you can provide enough champagne for your crew to drink our health, I will be more than grateful."

"I am sure they would be delighted. I will come to you in an hour's time. As we stop at Malta tomorrow we will not be in Greece for at least four days."

"Thank you again for your kindness, Captain."

The Prince walked back to their cabin to find that in his absence Sacia had put on one of her new dresses.

It was of course the white one and he thought that no one could look more entrancing or more gracious.

"I had nothing to wear on my head," she said, "but I asked our Steward and he kindly brought me these white roses. There are not enough to make a wreath, but if I pin them on either side of my face I think I will look a bride!"

"You will look so lovely, beautiful and utterly and completely adorable. There is nothing more I could say except, my darling, that I love you with all my heart and I realise that I am the happiest and luckiest man in the whole wide world."

He was kissing her again.

And only when she was able to speak, did she ask,

"We don't have to tell the Captain our real names?"

"I once attended an English wedding, which took place on a ship, of a man who was at school with me. The only thing that counted was their Christian names. Thus you must give the Captain all your Christian names and I will give him mine. Although we will sign the Register under a false surname, what really will matter is that our

Christian names are correct. Anyway no one, once we are married, will dare to suggest that it's not legal."

"Are you quite sure?" Sacia asked in a small voice and he knew it troubled her.

"I promise you that I am absolutely correct in all I have told you. Now tell me your names."

With a little hesitation as if she was still nervous, Sacia muttered,

"I was Christened Maria, Christa, Sacia, and I have always been called Sacia because it was easier for me to say when I was little."

The Prince smiled.

"I am sure it will impress the Captain that we are of considerable consequence. Now my Christian names are Nicolo, Murar, Alexander."

"He will certainly be impressed with those," Sacia laughed, "and of course he believes you to be a Count."

"Which I hope he will go on believing."

Then he changed the conversation quickly.

Naturally he was well aware that Sacia was curious about him just as he was curious about her, but he knew it would spoil their honeymoon if they even began to think about the future.

He did not want to contemplate the difficulties of appeasing not only her family but his Prime Minister and Cabinet.

So instead of speaking he put his arms round Sacia once again.

And he kissed her until once again they were flying up into the sky.

*

Later on that night Sacia moved against him and he pulled her a little closer to him.

"Do you still love me?" he asked tenderly. "And I have not hurt or frightened you?"

"I love you, Nico," Sacia sighed. "I did not know how wonderful love was until you gave me all I dreamt of and longed for and thought it would never happen to me."

"But it happened and now you know, my precious one, that Aphrodite has blessed us and nothing and no one could ever keep us apart. And we will never lose the love we have now for each other."

As he spoke to her, he reflected on the strange little Marriage Service the Captain had conducted.

It was as Holy to them both as if it had taken place in a great Cathedral.

The Captain had ended making them husband and wife with the words,

"With the power invested in me by Her Majesty Queen Victoria of Great Britain I now pronounce you man and wife and may God bless your union."

He made them, the Prince then thought, completely united with each other and the vows that came from their hearts could never be broken.

"I love you, Nico," Sacia whispered to him again.

As the Prince's lips sought hers, he said from the very depth of his heart and his soul,

"I love you, my precious, adorable and beautiful wife, I adore you for ever and ever."

CHAPTER SEVEN

"It has been so wonderful!" Sacia exclaimed. "I think today was the best of them all."

The Prince thought so too.

He had taken her to every possible place in Greece that was remotely connected with Aphrodite.

He sensed at every site as if they were in a wholly vibrant atmosphere that came from Aphrodite herself.

Because he loved Sacia with his whole heart and she loved him, he felt that their lovemaking was Divine, as if they were on Mount Olympus with the Gods.

It was indeed, the Prince recognised, the love he had always sought and the love he could never find.

Yet like a miracle it had now happened to him.

Nothing could be more marvellous or wonderful than the love Sacia gave him and he gave her.

It was impossible for either of them to think or speak of anything but love and Aphrodite.

They went up Mount Hyrrettus overlooking Athens where there was a spring where women drank who wished to have a child.

Sacia looked at the Prince as he told her about it and then without saying anything she had gone down on her knees to drink a little of the water.

Because it was a moment of Holiness and purity, neither of them spoke.

They saw many marble statues of Aphrodite, but to both of them the effigies had little to do with the feelings within them.

The Goddess was obviously blessing them both as she had brought them together in the first place.

Of course they had discussed Aphrodite in detail.

The Prince had read more about her than Sacia and he related to her how the ancient Greeks believed she was the daughter of Zeus by the shadowy Goddess Dione and she was also thought to have sprung from the foam of the sea.

Scholars of mythology had written that Aphrodite was the child of 'the earth and the sky'. And it was the sky which with thunder and lightning sends down the rain of fruitfulness for mankind.

What struck them was the light in Greece, which they realised was so different from the light anywhere else in the world. It seemed to make the very air they breathed purer than any they had ever known.

As the Prince told her, the Greeks were never tired of describing the appearance of this light, as the Goddess of Love was a young virgin rising out of the waves with the light from the foam making a background for her body – and that made her so different from every other Goddess and every woman who had ever tried to emulate her.

They wandered around hand in hand from Temple to shrine.

At times the Prince found himself talking to Sacia as if she was a man of his own age and he realised that her replies and questions were more intelligent than a man's would have been.

He found it hard to understand just how anyone so young and beautiful could be so astute and perceptive.

It made him appreciate that he could never be bored with her as he had been with the women he had had a passing *affaire de coeur* with.

For Sacia the wonder of Nico and his love made her feel as if she was still in a dream – it could not really be happening to her.

The second night they were together, she whispered softly against the Prince's shoulder and he knew, as she quoted the famous words of the poet Sophocles, that they came from her heart.

"Many marvels there are, but none as marvellous as man.

Over the dark he rides in the teeth of the Winter's Storm."

"But not a winter's storm for us," she added. "But storms we both ran away from."

The Prince did not answer, because he did not want her to worry about what they had left behind or what they were to face in the future.

He merely kissed her until they were floating in the foam of Aphrodite and then moving into the sky towards the Milky Way.

*

It was three weeks after they had arrived in Athens and had travelled over a great deal of Greece before the Prince took Sacia to Delphi.

This he had kept to the last because he thought it was the most significant of all the places for her to visit and he recognised mournfully that their honeymoon must come to an end soon.

It was from Delphi that they would return to the world that was no longer a part of the Goddess Aphrodite.

It was a sunny day.

As they walked up to the shining cliffs the haunting view beneath them was breathtakingly perfect.

There was the faint blue of the sea in the distance and the valley of the grey-blue olive trees below and the blue mountains to the left and right with the shining cliffs rising behind them.

There was a quietness and a mystery in the air that was impossible to describe.

And once again the Prince knew it was Aphrodite blessing them. She had brought them together and now she joined them even closer in their love for each other.

They sat down on some fallen marble and, holding Sacia by the hand, the Prince told her,

"Apollo chose to land here first when he came to Greece. As he sprang out onto the land from the sea, he announced that he took for himself the beauty and wonder of this place – and it became his."

"I can understand him desiring it," Sacia pondered. "Yet, however handsome and wonderful Apollo was, he could not be as marvellous as *you*, my Nico!"

The Prince drew her a little closer.

"I can only pray that you will go through our lives together still thinking that. I knew when I found you that there could never be anyone else to equal you or as divine as you are."

"But then you did not love me at first, Nico. I think that I loved you from the very first moment you drove the gondola away down the canal so that I could not be seen by anyone looking out of the windows."

The Prince smiled.

"I think, actually, my lovely one, you succeed more than you think in expressing your feelings. I have never in my whole life talked to someone who could tell me exactly what I wanted to hear in words that are as beautiful as you are yourself."

She put out her hands to touch his face.

"I love you! I adore you, Nico. Must we go back to reality? I want to stay here for ever and just dream my life away in your arms."

"That is what I want too, but unfortunately I have obligations, and you, of all people, would not expect me to disappoint those who rely on me."

"No, of course not!"

Then in a small trembling voice, Sacia added,

"Suppose they don't like me?"

"They will love you because you are beautiful," the Prince answered. "And remember, too, that wherever we go the Blessing of Aphrodite will go with us."

"Are you quite sure?" Sacia asked.

"Absolutely sure," he insisted firmly.

They then explored the shining cliffs and the Prince showed her where the Oracle had been which the pilgrims consulted and how the words from the lips of Priests were carried out into the world outside.

The wonder and beauty of the sunshine seemed to blind their eyes and they felt as if they were listening in their hearts to the prophetic words of the Oracle.

It told them that they should be brave and strong for the daunting tasks that lay ahead of them and also that they would succeed in helping other people as they themselves had been helped.

The message was very clear and yet, because they were so close, there was no need for either the Prince or Sacia to attempt to translate it into words.

Then in silence they rode back down the hill on the donkeys that had taken them up to the cliffs.

The Prince recognised that he was now leaving the ancient Gods for the real world in which he and Sacia had to survive in the future.

*

He had left her one morning when they were in Athens and went to the Italian Embassy and sent a message to Texxo to be ready for his return.

163

He told him to say nothing of what had happened or where he had been since they left Vienz and that he was writing to the Lord Chamberlain to prepare him in great confidence for the day of his homecoming.

He had also, while he was at the Embassy, asked if they knew of any yacht he could charter, as he wished to be taken to Venice.

He did not specify that he actually intended to stop before Venice at a point where Vienz had a narrow outlet to the sea.

That he would have to sail up the Adriatic made the Embassy Officials realise that he required a large yacht.

He did not use his Royal title, but one of his others, which made them aware he was of some consequence.

Eventually they contacted a rich Greek, who owned a very comfortable yacht that he occasionally hired out to wealthy visitors who wished to explore the islands.

The Prince had been delighted at his agreement and he was determined never again to encounter the rowdy young men who had upset Sacia on their voyage to Rome.

He asked if the yacht could be available in three days time and had taken it first to carry them to Delphi.

Sacia had been thrilled when she heard that he had hired it and admitted that she had been dreading being on the same type of ship they had travelled on previously.

The yacht was very up-to-date and the crew, who were all Greeks, were most obliging.

The Master cabin was exceedingly comfortable and it was even more luxurious than their cabin on the English ship that had brought them to Athens.

The Prince had asked at the Embassy if they would arrange to have flowers sent to the yacht before he and his wife arrived as he wanted a display arranged in the Master cabin.

Everything had been done according to his request.

He had, after some consideration, decided that he must inform his Lord Chamberlain at the Palace in Vienz that he was returning.

He was well aware that by this time they would be extremely anxious as to what had happened to him and he thought it would be a mistake for him to appear suddenly without warning them he was on his way.

He had sat in the Embassy puzzling as to what he would say and finally he wrote to the Lord Chamberlain,

"I am instructed to inform you that the gentleman, who has for some time now been missing, will be arriving by sea in about ten days. Please make arrangements for him to be met, but no one except yourself is to be aware that it is he who is returning."

The Prince did not sign the letter and, although the Secretary at the Embassy had looked at the address with surprise, he had been too diplomatic to ask any questions.

He had only commented,

"I believe Vienz, sir, is very near to Venice!"

"You are quite right," replied the Prince, "and it is as a matter of fact a very attractive country."

"I hope I shall have the opportunity to visit it some day," the Secretary remarked.

"I feel sure you will find it a delightful country to visit, but it does not boast the great history and traditions they have here in Greece."

The Prince then thanked him profusely for making the arrangements about the yacht.

When he went back to Sacia, who was waiting for him anxiously in the hotel, she had jumped up as soon as he appeared and flung her arms round him.

"You have been away a long time, Nico. I was half afraid you had forgotten me."

"Do you really think that possible, Sacia?"

He had kissed her with what he meant to be just a kiss of happiness, but instead it became one of passion and fire.

He then carried her to the bed and made her know without words how much she meant to him and how it was impossible for them ever to be parted.

*

Now they were riding together down through the olive trees to the little port where their yacht was waiting for them.

When they reached the yacht it was already time to change for dinner and they discussed all they had seen that day.

It was most fortunate that the Greek who owned the yacht employed a French chef and the food, since he was given *carte blanche* by the Prince, was not only delicious but original.

There was a Greek wine to drink that the Prince had always enjoyed and which Sacia found an elixir.

The Prince felt that she did not realise they were moving away from Greece and into the Adriatic and when they anchored a little later in a quiet bay, the Prince took her down to the Master cabin.

He had underrated Sacia's perceptiveness.

"I think, darling," she murmured, "you don't want me to say 'goodbye' to Greece. I know we have already left it, but promise me we will come back again one day!"

"Of course we will, Sacia, and we will teach our children almost from the moment they are born about the Greek Gods and Goddesses and how influential they have been in both our lives."

"I know," Sacia said quietly, "that you were sent to me by the Goddess Aphrodite and that our children will each have a special God to protect them and make them as happy as we are."

The Prince kissed her as there was no need for any further discussion.

*

The next day and the day after they talked about themselves, their love and the wisdom of the Greek fathers.

167

They were both aware that they were avoiding the moment when they would have to explain to one another who they really were.

They recognised only too well the difficulties that could arise – difficulties that might easily sweep away the happiness of the dream-world they were still living in.

When they were only a short distance from the Port of Vienz where they were to disembark, the Prince sent for the Captain.

He told him he wished to arrive at eleven o'clock the following day and they would therefore anchor in some quiet bay for the night as there would be no hurry for them to leave the following morning.

The Captain was wise enough to ask no questions, but just to do as he was told.

He found a delightful bay. There were cliffs rising straight out of the sea that would prevent any inquisitive sightseers from observing them.

After dinner they went out on deck to admire the moonlight shining silvery on the calm sea and millions of stars were coming out overhead.

"I know, my darling husband," said Sacia, "that you are thinking of me and not speaking of what lies ahead. But as we are to arrive tomorrow, I have to know who you are and to tell you who I am."

"I can only tell you that you are the most wonderful and perfect woman in the whole world," the Prince replied. "I am not really concerned with who your parents are."

He paused before he continued,

168

"But, as you say, we have to know the truth about each other and, although this might upset you a little, we will have to be married again."

Sacia stared at him.

"*Married again*? But you told me our marriage was legal!"

"It was completely and absolutely legal. But at the same time I cannot deprive my people of the happiness and joy of a wedding."

There was silence for a while and then Sacia asked,

"*Your* people?"

"I am Prince Nicolo of Vienz."

Again there was a silence.

Then to his astonishment Sacia gave a little cry of delight.

"Prince Nicolo!" she exclaimed. "I have heard of you and, as you are Royal, Papa will be delighted."

The Prince stared at her.

"Why should he be?"

"Because, as I told you, Papa wanted me to marry somebody of great consequence. He had chosen a terrible and ghastly man who is King of Brankestoff."

She paused before continuing,

"It is a tiny German Kingdom and he is a very big and horrible man. That was why I tried to drown myself."

The Prince felt bewildered, but he put his arms around her.

"Are you telling me that your father expected you to marry a King? In that case, *who* is he?"

"Although they live in Venice Papa is the Archduke Otto of Austria and Mama is the second daughter of King Ferdinand II of Naples. So you can understand why they wanted me to be a Queen!"

For a moment the Prince could not find his voice.

He had been so certain in his own mind that Sacia came perhaps from an influential family, but there was no Royalty in Venice because it was a Republic.

Now he knew that only the Gods could have been so unbelievably kind to him.

If Sacia's father was an Archduke, it meant he was a son of the Emperor of Austria.

Every male member of their Royal Family had the title of Archduke and their daughters were Princesses, and in Italy through her mother Sacia would be a Principessa.

For a moment he could hardly believe that this was true and he was not dreaming.

Nothing could be better for his country.

If his wife's father was Austrian that country would never attempt to absorb his and the Italians would respect Vienz because the Ruling Princess was the granddaughter of one of their Kings.

He could hardly take it in that he had been so lucky.

He could only gaze at Sacia in wonderment.

"I was so afraid," she said softly, "that Papa would be angry if I had refused someone Royal for someone he would think of as a 'commoner', but *you* are Royal! So he will, I know, be delighted.

"We will certainly invite him and your mother to our wedding!"

Then he was kissing her almost reverently as in his heart he acknowledged how Aphrodite had bequeathed to them everything they could have possibly desired on earth.

*

They arrived promptly at the small Port of Vienz the following morning at eleven o'clock.

When the Prince looked out of the porthole, he saw waiting for him not just his Lord Chamberlain but four troopers from his favourite Cavalry Regiment.

The Lord Chamberlain came aboard and the Prince shook him warmly by the hand.

"I am really delighted to see Your Royal Highness back," the Lord Chamberlain said. "We were becoming increasingly worried as to what had happened to you."

"I was afraid of that, but do tell me first, what is happening at the Palace," the Prince answered.

The Lord Chamberlain knew, without his putting it into words, exactly what the question meant.

He replied,

"I don't think it should upset Your Royal Highness, but Princess Marziale of Bassanz returned home and Ruta, who you kindly made a Duke, went with her."

He paused for a moment and smiled, as he went on,

"We were informed a week ago that their marriage had been announced."

171

"That is exactly what I wanted to hear. I feel sure they will be very happy."

The Lord Chamberlain smiled again and the Prince was certain that he had guessed the real reason why he had made Ruta a Duke and then run away himself.

"You will understand, Your Royal Highness," he said, "that the Prime Minister is very perturbed about it and is now looking through the *Almanac de Gotha* to find you another suitable wife."

"I would hate him to waste his time," the Prince replied. "In fact I have brought my fiancée with me!"

The Lord Chamberlain's eyes now widened and the Prince realised it was news he had not expected.

"*Your fiancée!*" he exclaimed.

"I must let you into a secret. I have found someone whom I love and who loves me. As she also had run away from an arranged marriage that would have been unhappy, we were incredibly fortunate to find each other under the most bizarre circumstances."

There was just a perceptible pause before the Lord Chamberlain, a little anxiously, asked,

"Will Your Royal Highness tell me the name of this extremely fortunate lady?"

The Prince was much enjoying this conversation as he had expected.

Slowly he explained,

"Her name is Sacia and she is a Princess! Her father is Archduke Otto of Austria and her mother is the second daughter of the late King Ferdinand II of Naples."

He thought that if the Lord Chamberlain had not been so well trained, his jaw would have dropped open from sheer astonishment.

"I congratulate Your Royal Highness," he managed to blurt out. "I cannot imagine anyone more suitable to be your bride and it will be a delight, as Your Royal Highness well knows, for the Prime Minister and all the Cabinet to dance at your wedding."

The Prince laughed and it was a very happy sound.

"I am certain they will and I shall be dancing too, But it is vital that we should be married immediately!

"What I would like you to do is to go back at once and make all the necessary arrangements for our reception when we arrive. Then bring back two Ladies-in-Waiting for Princess Sacia in two days time."

The Lord Chamberlain nodded.

"In the meantime will you communicate with her father and mother in Venice and arrange for them to be in the Palace for our arrival?"

The Lord Chamberlain laughed as if he could not help it.

"Your Royal Highness always springs a surprise on us when we least expect it. Of course I quite understand that it is important for no one to know that you have been alone together and unchaperoned."

"I have not said that!" the Prince replied. "But it happens to be true!"

"Is the marriage to take place just as soon as the Princess's family arrive?" the Lord Chamberlain asked.

"Naturally and before they can make trouble and upset her by saying that she should not have run away."

"Was it for the same reason Your Royal Highness left us?" the Lord Chamberlain enquired a little cheekily.

"Yes! They wanted her to marry a minor German King who was years older than her. They thought it was essential for her to sit on a Royal throne."

"Well, even the Prime Minister could not have thought of anyone so satisfactory from our country's point of view. I can only commend Your Royal Highness for being exceedingly clever and tell you without reservation that this will be a great source of strength for Vienz."

"That is exactly what I thought myself, but actually when you see Sacia you will realise that I am not merely clever, as you have just said, but the happiest man in the whole world."

"What I will do, if Your Royal Highness agrees, is to return at once to the Palace, taking only one trooper with me as a bodyguard. I will leave the other three to attend to you here and everything will be in order in two days time."

"We will arrive the night before the wedding and you must arrange for the Princess's family to be at the Palace waiting for her."

"I will send a carriage and a Cavalry Escort to Venice at dawn tomorrow morning," the Lord Chamberlain promised, "and that should give them time to dress, leave in the afternoon and have a quiet night before you arrive."

"And the wedding?"

"I will arrange it at the Cathedral and Your Royal Highness's people will start decorating the streets at dawn. I presume you will want to have fireworks and all the usual entertainments they always expect?"

"Double what they expect! I shall enjoy them all myself. As I have already told you, I am a very very happy man!"

"You can imagine I am very curious, Your Royal Highness, to see how anyone can have captivated you, if that is really the right word, so completely," the Lord Chamberlain pronounced.

"You will not be in the least surprised when you see Princess Sacia – "

He insisted that the Lord Chamberlain should have something to eat and drink before he left and he continued talking to him while he was doing so.

All this time he had told Sacia to remain in her cabin.

"I don't want anyone to see you," he insisted, "until you appear officially as my fiancée and the future Royal Ruler, with me, of Vienz. Then when they do finally see you, they will be overjoyed and completely overcome by your beauty and grace."

He smiled at her as he carried on,

"It will give them something to think about without worrying us with uncomfortable and difficult questions."

Sacia laughed.

"You think of everything, Nico. I only hope your people will love me and not take a violent dislike to me."

"No one could possibly ever dislike you, they have been on their knees begging me to be married for at least five years. So they will receive you with open arms and it will be up to you to make them love you as much as I do."

"You know what I really want to do, my darling, is to love you and help you to be the greatest Ruler of your Principality there has ever been."

The Prince thought, but did not say so, that it would be thanks to Sacia if he was not deposed if ever the dangers threatened that everyone had foreseen.

All that mattered was that she was his and once they were married in the Cathedral of Vienz there would be no question of his being badgered to marry anyone else.

"I love you! I adore you!" he cried when the Lord Chamberlain had departed.

He had told the Captain to move the yacht a little way out to sea.

"Tell the Escort we will be back in the evening! But now we just want to be alone in the sea with only the mermaids to stare at us."

The Captain laughed.

"I think, sir, considering how beautiful your wife is, it is more likely to be *mermen* taking a peep at her!"

The Prince laughed too and he thought it somewhat amusing that the Captain still had no idea that he was of any particular consequence. He would have assumed that the Cavalry Escort belonged to the Lord Chamberlain.

They moved out into the Adriatic, just far enough to be out of sight both of Vienz and Italy.

"Now my darling," the Prince sighed, "we are alone again and for the moment unimportant. We can look back and think how astute we both were to run away as we did and find each other.

"I wanted to be an ordinary man and as an ordinary man to find the true love I have always believed was only written about by poets and dreamt about by people like myself – and which would never actually materialise."

Sacia gave a little laugh.

"Do you really think you could ever be an ordinary man?" she asked him. "You are extraordinary, unique and unlike any other man who has ever been born. I love you, my Nico, because you will never become ordinary, but will remain extraordinary for ever."

The Prince blushed at her words, picked her up in his arms and carried her towards the bed.

"As an extraordinary man, I am going to make love to an extraordinary woman. We both know that we have been totally blessed by the Gods and Goddesses of Greece and in particular by Aphrodite herself, who has made our love Divine."

His voice deepened as he went on,

"It will carry us up into the sky and we will never, either of us, ever run away again."

Sacia laughed and then before the Prince could kiss her, she replied,

"I love you! I will love you for ever! That is a vow that will never be broken and I am certain, my wonderful, exceptional and very handsome husband that if Aphrodite is listening, she will bless us and keep us in love with each other, not only for this world, but for all Eternity."

The Prince drew her closer to him still and then he was evoking in her the sacred emotion of Love.

It came from Aphrodite and has inspired men and women since the beginning of time.

It is a love that is not only physical but spiritual.

It has sprung directly from the Gods and Goddesses of Greece and from God himself.

God has made mankind in His image and has given them on earth, if they sought for it, the Glory which is in Heaven.

Made in the USA
Middletown, DE
19 April 2023